# THE LIE

# THAT

# BINDS

## By
## Linda Jackson

*Story idea and cover design*
*by Jeffery Jackson*

Library of Congress Control Number: 2001119921

ISBN 0-9716442-0-9

Printed in the U.S.A.
Jackson Publishing
7661 Forstoria Cove
Southaven, Mississippi 38672

**Please visit us online at
www.jacksonbooks.com**

# *Acknowledgments*

I am very grateful to my friend and husband Jeff for his untiring encouragement during the writing and publication of this book. Without his support, my writing would have continued to exist only as a "dream." Thanks for "a dream come true."

Thanks also to all of my family and friends who support and encourage my writing.

A special thanks goes to my daughters Olivia and Chloe who encourage me by writing stories of their own.

# One

Perspiration rolled down the sides of his face and soaked the worn collar of his T-shirt as seven-year-old Joshua Tanner hurried through the waist-high weeds that led to the pond. Every summer since Joshua was four, he had watched the older boys in the housing project disappear into the woods in the afternoon. And since he was four, Joshua had longed to join them. But two things stood in his way – his age and his "Grandma." The older boys insisted he was "too little", and his grandma insisted it was "too dangerous." Today Joshua decided he was tired of both excuses. He didn't think it was fair to watch another summer go by and not be able to go into the woods and swim in the pond with the big boys. Besides he was tired of watching "Oprah" with his grandma.

Anticipation conquered Joshua, propelling his scrawny legs along the dusty path. "Terrence will be so surprised to see me," he said excitedly. "I'll show them I'm big enough. I can swim better than all of 'em," he said panting, grass whipping his bare legs. "I swim in the tub every night 'til Grandma makes me get out."

Joshua had heard plenty of stories about the pond from his grandma and her church friends. Stories of little boys drowning in the pond or getting eaten by bears in the woods were supposed to scare him, but it would take more than a few stories from some old ladies to keep a curious seven-year-old away from an adventure.

"Grandma always wants me to stay in the house," Joshua grumbled. "Always talking 'bout it's too hot or somebody might snatch me and kidnap me. I'll be glad when my mama comes back to get me," he said, his running now turning into a very slow jog. "I bet they got real swimming pools up in Chicago, and I can go swimming any time I want."

Joshua slowed his pace to a walk when he heard the sounds of big trucks on the highway, an indication that he was nearing the pond. He stopped and peeped through the tall grass. Several feet ahead of him was a small bare stretch of land that he mistook for a beach. And beyond the beach lay the famous Ecky's Pond.

Rays of sunlight glared through the large trees and rested on the pond. Two muddy-white ducks glided gracefully across the water while frogs leaped along the edge. A gentle breeze carried the scent of honeysuckle through the air. Joshua took a deep breath. He wanted to remember every detail of his first trip to the pond.

Not wanting to be discovered too soon and sent back home, Joshua crouched behind a bush to wait until the older boys were in the water. "Where are they?" he whispered when he didn't see them near the water. He quietly inched his way behind another bush with a better view of the pond. Then he saw them. At first he only saw the four boys huddled in a semi-circle. Then he saw the girl. She was lying a few feet away from the pond. Her bright yellow tank top was covered with blood.

Then Joshua saw the knife. One of the boys clutched it securely in his blood-soaked hand. Joshua's spine tingled and his stomach flipped. His legs went numb. He wanted to run, but his legs wouldn't respond. His eyes were glued to the scene at the pond. Then it was too late – the boys started running toward the path. Joshua now wished he had listened to his grandmother. Joshua knew he had to hide, and quickly. He stooped lower and tried to crawl under a larger bush. A loose branch caught his shoe. He tried desperately to shake himself loose, but the noisy bush only caused commotion. Joshua tried to get up and run, but his legs felt paralyzed. He fell to the ground and lay on his stomach as he heard heavy feet running his way. He dropped his face into the grass. He was doomed.

One of the boys grabbed Joshua by the collar and yanked him to his feet. "What are you doing out here, you little punk?" His nails were cutting into Joshua's throat. Tears streamed down Joshua's face as he stared into the cold eyes of Allen Smith, a known delinquent infamous for robbing a convenience store.

"I...I was going for a swim. I didn't see nothing. I swear," Joshua muttered.

The boys looked at one another. "What do you mean you didn't see nothing?" Terrence, Joshua's trusted neighbor, asked.

Fear paralyzed Joshua. This was not the same Terrence who protected him on the playground occasionally. This was the Terrence he'd seen riding in the backseat of a squad car on Saturday nights. "I just got here, I swear. I saw y'all standing by the pond and I tried to run home," Joshua answered with his fingers crossed behind his back.

Terrence slapped Joshua across the mouth. Joshua shrieked in pain and stumbled backwards onto a bush. Blood spurted from his mouth.

"You're the little snitch who ratted us out to the cops about the cigarettes we stole from Circle K!" yelled Ron, an ex-gang member who had recently moved to Mississippi from "up North."

"N-n-no I didn't," Joshua stuttered, keeping his fingers crossed. "That was Marvin. Yeah, Marvin told on you. Not me. And I won't tell nothing this time either."

"You're lying, you little rat," Ron said as he gave Joshua's side a feel of his size 11 Nike. Joshua screamed and curled into a fetal position. "I won't tell nothing. Just leave me alone," he sobbed.

"I thought you didn't see anything," Ron said, his voice intimidating.

"I mean I won't tell nobody you beat me up. Please just let me go home," begged Joshua. "My grandma will be looking for me." Joshua wrapped his arms tightly around his stomach. Through his window of tears he could see the four boys towering over him. Fear and anxiety also covered their faces. Joshua now wished he hadn't lied to his grandmother about going to play at Marvin's. If only he had told the truth, she would have stopped him from going and he wouldn't be in this mess.

"What are we gonna do with him?" asked Jay, a red-haired, freckled kid who was plagued by paranoia. Both his voice and his body were shaking.

Terrence glanced around the woods as if looking for an answer. He was at least four inches taller than the other boys, which made him look older than his fourteen years. His childish muscles had begun to bulge slightly, and a thin mustache was trying to break through to add maturity to his face. "We can't let him leave. He'll run straight home and tell his grandma everything. We have to get rid of him," he said without emotion.

"No, I won't. I promise," Joshua pleaded. He began to cry harder and louder. He wasn't ready to die. He had always wanted to go to Six Flags in Atlanta, or at least travel outside of Mississippi.

"Please don't hurt me guys," he begged. "I'll do anything you ask. Just let me live."

"Come on, Terrence," said Jay, his voice still shaky and weak. "We're already in a lot of trouble."

"We'll be in even more trouble if we let him leave here," said Terrence.

So gripped by terror, Joshua wasn't aware that his pants were soaked. His mind was on the knife in Ron's hand and on how he could somehow get on Terrence's good side again. "Terrence, I've never done nothing bad to you," he argued. "Why would you want to hurt me?"

Terrence didn't answer.

"I don't want to die, Terrence," Joshua muttered again.

"You should've thought of that before you came out here," said Ron the gangbanger. "I say we drown him," he told the others. "It'll look like an accident."

"Come on, guys. He's just a little kid," Jay said with a nervous laugh. "We can give him money or something. He'll keep quiet."

"That's what you said about Sandy," snapped Allen.

"I'll be quiet. I promise," Joshua said with a desperate voice. "I won't be like her. Girls always talk too much. Boys don't."

"Sorry, kid, you can't be trusted either," said Ron. "Little kids have bigger mouths than girls."

"I can be trusted," Joshua said hurriedly. "Please, Terrence, I promise I can be trusted this time. You know I won't say nothing."

Terrence looked toward the pond. "Let's just get this over with," he said.


Joshua resisted all the way to the pond. He thought about all the lies he'd told and how his grandmother kept warning him about the devil coming after children who lied a lot. The devil had come to get him.

Joshua was petrified when his body hit the dingy water. A scream echoed through the woods as Joshua's head was buried under the water. He instinctively held his breath in defense against the clutches of death. It wasn't long before his luck ran out, and the murky water began to seep into his nostrils. Joshua began to cough as the water engulfed his nostrils and throat. The kicks from his scrawny legs were no match for the grips of the teenagers. Joshua stopped struggling.

Jay Stringer stared at the still body he was holding under the water. "He's dead!" he yelled with a frantic voice. "He's dead!" He began to sob loudly. Jay's head was light and his stomach knotted. "We've gotta do something!" he screamed. His voice was wild. Jay snatched the lifeless body away from Ron and cradled the seven-year-old like a baby as he hurriedly waded out of the pond. He placed the body on the ground and began to try to resuscitate it.

"What are you doing!" yelled Ron. "He's dead, man, you should've left him in the pond!"

"Let's just get out of here!" Allen screamed deliriously.

"We can't just leave them like this!" cried Jay.

"It's over, Jay," Terrence said. "Joshua's dead, and so is Sandy. Now let's just go before anybody else comes out here."

Jay didn't move. He just kneeled beside Joshua's body as he rocked back and forth and sobbed. "What have we done?" he moaned as he buried his face into his palms.

# TWO

Rita Stringer worked hard all day at the Pancake House Restaurant and looked forward to resting with her feet up at the end of the day. After nine hours of grinning at patrons who barely left her a five- percent tip, Rita was almost glad to step through the door of her dingy little apartment in the projects. But she still hadn't decided which was worse – her stingy customers or her shabby excuse of a dwelling place. The worn tan-shaded carpet always needed cleaning, but never got it. The yellowing white walls screamed for a fresh coat of paint. The shabby thrift store furniture – a plaid three-legged couch with a Campbell's soup can under one end, a threadbare recliner that no longer reclined, and a cat-clawed coffee table that served as an "antique" – only added to the room's sadness.

Rita was only thirty-three, but she looked fifty-three. Gray streaks had invaded her auburn hair, and fine lines surrounded her tired eyes. She had no laugh lines because she never laughed. In fact, she rarely smiled. She had lived a hard life, to say the least. Married at sixteen then divorced at twenty with three small boys to raise, she felt that fate had certainly dealt her a bad hand. She had a lousy job as a waitress, an ex-husband who refused to pay child support, two sons in juvenile detention, and one son who seemed to be headed the same way.

She constantly worried about her son Jay. He was basically a good kid, but he hung out with a bad crowd and he performed poorly in school. During the summer he was left to himself all day while Rita worked, and she could only imagine what he might get himself into.

Her shift at the restaurant ended at four, and she expected Jay to be at home waiting for her when she got there fifteen minutes later. But that Thursday afternoon he wasn't. The apartment was empty, and there was no note from Jay stating where he was. Rita knew that he normally went into the woods every afternoon with a few other boys, but he was always home before she got there.

She didn't think much of it, however. It was only normal that a fourteen-year-old boy would come home a little later than usual every now and then. So she continued with her daily afternoon ritual of changing out of her uniform and into her frayed blue jeans and her favorite Abercrombie and Fitch T-shirt that she had purchased at a garage sale. She grabbed a glass of Kool-Aid then reclined on the sofa to watch a talk show, hoping she'd feel better by watching other people who had made dumber mistakes than herself.

The knock at the door startled Rita, and she nearly dropped her glass. It had been less than a year ago when the police appeared at her door one afternoon to haul her oldest son Darrell off to jail for drug possession. Rumors had floated around town that someone was selling drugs out of one of the apartments at the Roseville Housing Project. Without hesitation the police sought out the Stringer unit because of the Stringer boys' questionable reputation. They found Darrell's stash in his bedroom closet. A few months later the police returned. This time for Stephen, Rita's middle son.

Rita prayed that Jay would not get involved in the same dealings as his brothers. She even started attending a church to make her prayers legitimate. It seemed to be working so far. Jay had not gotten into any serious trouble yet.

Rita opened the door and froze when she saw the bewildered faces of Terrence, Allen, and Ron and Jay's limp body propped upon their shoulders.

"What's happened to Jay!" she screamed as she gathered the strength to grab her son around the waist and drag his body to the sofa. Jay's breathing was shallow and hurried. His skin was clammy and so pale that is was almost colorless. His eyes were fixed into a wild stare.

"What's wrong with him!" Rita yelled as she fell on the floor beside the sofa and cradled Jay's head in her arms. "One of you dial 9-1-1!"

Allen and Ron looked at Terrence. Terrence picked up the phone on the kitchen wall and dialed 9-1-1. When Rita heard the words "bitten by a water moccasin" she screamed again.

"A moccasin! They're poisonous!" She looked from face to face for answers.

"The ambulance is on the way," said Terrence. "They said to prop his feet up on pillows and keep him covered with a blanket until they get here."

"Where was he bitten?" Rita asked as she frantically searched Jay's arms and legs for a snakebite.

"Right here," answered Terrence as he lifted Jay's shirt and pointed to a red swollen cut on Jay's side. "Ron used his knife to try to get the poison out."

Ron nodded in agreement.

"Oh, God, have mercy on my child," Rita began to sob. "I can't lose Jay. He's all I have."

Jay began to mumble. The only word Rita understood was "sorry."

Within minutes sirens blared throughout the neighborhood. People peeped through miniblinds while some gathered in the streets. Paramedics rushed into the apartment and placed Jay on a stretcher.

"He's in shock," one of them announced. "Good thing you called an ambulance. It's happening all over town. Kids out playing in the middle of the day in all this heat. Dehydrating like crazy. Add a snakebite to that and we got serious trouble. Jessica, we need oxygen and an IV," he said to his partner.

The three other boys eased out of the apartment unnoticed among the commotion. The paramedics carried Jay to the ambulance with Rita following. The ambulance sped off with its sirens blaring. The neighborhood watched and wondered.

———

Sadie Belle Brown thought that maybe it was time to give her grandson Joshua a call. It had been well past an hour since he left the apartment and said he was going to play with his friend Marvin across the street. Joshua knew that his time at other folks' homes was limited to an hour. Sadie Belle had taught him well about "wearing out his welcome." But when Sadie Belle called Marvin's apartment, Marvin's mother told her that Joshua hadn't been over and that she hadn't seen him all day. Sadie Belle's heart nearly stopped.

With bolts of fear shooting through her body, Sadie Belle began to comb every nook of the tiny two-bedroom apartment. Her mind had already known that she wouldn't find Joshua there, but her heart wouldn't let her stop searching. She screamed out his name as she peeped behind doors and under beds. She raced outside and looked around the apartment and up and down the street.

"Joshuuaa!" she yelled. "Joshuuaa!"

The playground was only a few yards from her apartment, but Sadie Belle couldn't tell whether any of the children playing was Joshua. She yelled toward the playground, "Joshuuaa!" There was no answer. Sadie Belle could feel her head about to explode with horrid thoughts of a kidnapping. Tears began to flow down her cheeks. Her hands shook uncontrollably. Sadie Belle ran back inside to call the police.

"So what do we do now?" asked Ron as he and his two comrades stood around the playground and watched the younger children play street ball.

"Just wait, I guess" Terrence answered with a shrug.

"Just wait!" Ron screamed. "Just how long do you think Jay is gonna be in shock? As soon as he comes out of it, he'll start telling his mama everything."

"Jay ain't stupid. I don't think he wants to join his brothers on their bus ride to Parchman," Terrence said angrily.

"He's the reason we're in all this mess in the first place," Allen snapped. "And he gets to lie around in a hospital and pretend he's in shock like the little kid in that movie about the client."

"He's not pretending," Terrence snapped back.

"Do you think we'll get sent to the state pen?" Ron asked nervously. He really could have used a cigarette at that moment, but he hadn't been able to sneak and buy any. His parents had been watching him like a hawk. He had started smoking when he was ten. One of his uncles on his mother's side of the family had taught him how. The same uncle had also let him have a beer or two by age ten. Moving to Mississippi from Saint Louis was rehab for Ron. He no longer had easy access to beer and cigarettes from his dysfunctional uncle. He now had to sneak and buy them with money he managed to earn from doing odd jobs for people around town. He was almost cured from his habits, but this incident was causing a setback.

"We're too young to go to prison," Terrence answered.

"Not if they try us as adults," added Allen.

"They won't try us as adults because we won't get caught," Terrence said with weak assurance.

"How can you be so sure?" asked Allen.

Terrence didn't answer. With the truth of the matter looming over his head, all he could do was stare at the playground. He began to think about little Joshua Tanner. He fought back the tears that had begun to sting his eyes. How could he have done such a thing to a little kid who probably would have been too scared to talk? But what if he had talked, Terrence wondered. What if Jay talks? Terrence felt as if a knife had been plunged through his stomach. Today had been worse than any nightmare he'd ever had.

"What we gonna do if they find out that Jay wasn't bitten by a snake?" asked Ron.

"We just tell them that we thought it was a snake, so you used your knife to get the poison out," answered Terrence.

"The knife!" yelled Allen. "We still have the knife!"

They all stood in dumbfounded silence. With the frenzy of commotion, they had not thought to hide the murder weapon.

"What are we gonna do now!" Allen yelled again. He had now begun to anxiously pace in a circle, his hands stuffed in the pockets of his oversized shorts. He had always believed he was stupid, at least that's what all the teachers said about him, but now he had committed the most stupid act in his life. It had been hard enough to live down the convenience store heists without adding a murder to his record.

"We can still get rid of the knife," said Terrence after a moment of thought. "If anybody asks about the knife used on Jay, we'll just get a different one."

"What if they know that the knife used on Jay was the same knife used on Sandy Cassin?" asked Ron.

"Don't be an idiot. This ain't TV," snapped Terrence. "Let's just try to calm down and don't do anything dumb."

"You mean dumber," said Allen.

"I say we make sure Jay doesn't rat us out," said Ron.

"What!" responded both Terrence and Allen.

"You're not thinking about—" Allen started but couldn't complete the absurd thought. "No way," he said, shaking his head, "Jay is our friend, Ron"

"Hey, it's his life or ours," Ron replied. "You saw him in the woods. He was freaked out. He's crazy enough to do anything."

Terrence had fallen silent again. He was lost in thought. He realized the danger they were in as long as Jay was in shock. The scene in the woods had convinced him of that. But how could they kill their own friend? They had gotten into this trouble because of their loyalty to Jay. He was the one Sandy Cassin had threatened, not the rest of them. They had gotten into serious trouble protecting Jay, now they contemplated killing him? Terrence shook his head from the thought.

"I'm going home," he said as he pulled away from the waist-high chain-linked fence that enclosed the playground. "I'll call the hospital and try to check on Jay."

Ron and Allen decided to go home also. Neither of the three knew what to expect at this point or what to do.

# THREE

Rita filled out forms at the front desk of the hospital's emergency entrance while paramedics wheeled Jay into a waiting area.

"Do you have insurance?" asked the receptionist.

"No," Rita replied. She self-consciously pulled a green card from her wallet and hurriedly handed it to the receptionist. She didn't need the whole hospital knowing that she was a welfare-to-work case.

"How long will he have to wait?" Rita asked.

"It'll only be a minute or so," answered the receptionist as she handed Rita her card and directed her to a waiting area.

Rita decided to stay by Jay's side as she tried to tune out the rest of the people waiting to see a doctor. None of their cases looked as serious as Jay's. A kid with a bruised knee screamed like a hungry baby. An elderly lady sat rubbing her leg. And a man with a dingy undershirt and blue jeans was reading "Sports Illustrated." Jay had slipped in and out of consciousness in the ambulance, and each time he had tried to tell Rita something that he was sorry about. He had mentioned Darrell and Stephen's names, but he had said nothing specific about them. Rita was just glad he was doing better. The paramedic had told her that Jay was out of danger but was still a little disoriented. Rita watched three other people come through the emergency room doors before a nurse and two orderlies came for Jay.

The nurse introduced herself as Beverly then led them into a large room that contained a myriad of beds sectioned off by drapes hanging from the ceiling. She then led them into one of the curtained areas, which contained only a bed and a tiny shelf. The cramped cubicle was barely large enough for the bed and shelf, but Rita and Beverly managed to squeeze inside as the orderlies lifted Jay onto the bed.

"What happened?" asked Beverly as she checked Jay's temperature.

"I'm not sure," Rita answered, fighting back tears. "His friends said he was bitten by a moccasin while he was swimming, then he blacked out."

"His temperature is normal," Beverly commented as she placed the thermometer into her pocket. She continued with checking Jay's blood pressure and taking a look at the snakebite.

"Why is he in and out of consciousness?" Rita asked. "Is this normal for a snake bite?"

"Some people go into shock from a bee sting or other insect bite. It's possible to go into shock from a snakebite. How did they know it was a moccasin?"

"I guess they just knew," Rita said with a shrug.

"He's lost quite a bit of blood. Did you get any details on how his friends got the poison out?" asked Beverly as she stared at Jay's paperwork and wrinkled her forehead into a concerned frown.

"No," Rita answered. "They just said that the kid named Ron used his knife."

"It looks like someone could have just taken a knife to his side and cut a little more than necessary," Beverly said matter-of-factly. "How long has he been unconscious?"

"He was unconscious when they brought him home around four thirty. Then he woke up in the ambulance and started mumbling."

"We'll keep his IV going and his feet elevated. He should regain full consciousness now that the bleeding has stopped. Dr. Glickman will be in shortly."

"Thank you," Rita responded. She was overcome with despair as Beverly closed the drape.

Rita dried her red eyes with a Kleenex from a box lying on the shelf in the examination area. Jay had not moved nor mumbled a sound since they had arrived at the hospital. The drape slid open, and the doctor entered.

"Hello, I'm Dr. Glickman," he said, extending his hand toward Rita. "Let's have a look at your boy here." He observed Jay's wound then checked the pupils of his eyes and touched his forehead. A disquieted frown covered his face. He motioned for Rita to follow him outside the draped area.

"His pupils look normal and his blood pressure has returned to normal," Dr. Glickman said in a near whisper. "All of his shock symptoms have disappeared except the unconsciousness, which concerns me."

Rita listened attentively.

"Beverly tells me that one of your son's friends used a knife to remove the venom from the snake bite."

Rita nodded.

"The cut from the knife looks unnecessarily deep in my opinion," said Dr. Glickman.

Rita's heart was beating rapidly. "What do you mean, Dr. Glickman?" she managed to ask in a shaky voice.

"The fact that your son has no other physical signs of shock except the unconsciousness leads me to believe that he may not still be in shock."

"You mean Jay is faking?" Rita asked with raised brows.

"I don't know," answered Dr. Glickman, still whispering. "If he is faking, then there must be a good reason for it."

Rita shuddered.

"I'd like to keep him in the hospital at least overnight, and I need you to stay with him."

"What about the other boys?" asked Rita. "Should I call any of them and see if they can tell me anymore?"

Dr. Glickman shook his head. "Not just yet. I'd like for Jay to talk to us himself."

Rita nodded and forced a smile. She was overwhelmed with disbelief. Her day had started out normal. She'd gotten up and had her usual cup of juice and a Pop Tart, read her morning devotional, treated her customers right, hadn't complained about the tips…now her son was in the hospital.

"He'll be fine," Dr. Glickman assured her as he patted her shoulder. "You just go on down to Admissions and fill out the paperwork. We'll handle the rest."

"Thank you, Dr. Glickman," Rita said very softly. "Thank you very much."

———

Ron tried to watch television, but the possibility of going to prison plagued his mind. He had seen his share of thugs, and the idea of being locked away with them was not appealing.

"What's the matter with you? You look like you just saw a spook or something," said Ron's father, Jimmy Lee, as he walked into the living room.

"Uh, nothing, sir," Ron answered.

"You sittin' in that chair fidgeting and carryin' on like the cat that ate the canary."

Ron remained silent. He dared not argue with his father, the strict disciplinarian who had kicked his own daughter out of the house when he found out she was pregnant. He was a self-employed auto mechanic who worked around the clock and was seldom home except to stop in for dinner, a time Ron hated. Jimmy Lee always made Ron feel uneasy. He constantly criticized him about everything, always reminding him of how worthless he was and that he would never amount to anything just like his dead-beat uncles on his mother's side.

There was a knock at the door, and Ron leaped to his feet to answer it before his father got up. He knew it would be Terrence and Allen. He opened the door slightly and squeezed outside before his father could say anything. Jimmy Lee considered Terrence a bad influence on Ron.

"What's up?" Ron asked his friends. "Have you heard anything about Jay?"

"I talked to his mama. She said they're keeping him in the hospital," Terrence answered.

"So, is he like talking or anything?" asked Ron.

"He's still unconscious," answered Terrence as he fidgeted with the cross he always wore around his neck. "The doctor thinks he'll wake up soon though, at least by the morning."

"Man, I can't believe this is happening!" Allen snapped angrily. "We did all we could to keep Sandy Cassin quiet. Now look where we're at?"

"Why don't you just chill, dude," replied Terrence. "Don't go psycho like Jay."

"What if Jay wakes up and tells everything?" Allen retorted.

"Yeah, man, I'm with Allen," Ron said to Terrence. "I think we should end this nightmare before Jay blows it for us."

"Dudes, you're losing it," said Terrence.

"Nah, Terrence, you're losing it," Ron replied angrily. "And you're stupid if you think we'll all live happily ever after. Jay is gonna wake up and he's gonna tell all about how Sandy Cassin tried to blackmail him and how we killed her and the little boy to keep him out of trouble."

Terrence turned his face away from Ron. He knew that Ron was right. Jail was inevitable unless they did the unthinkable. "I need some time to think," he responded.

"We don't have time to think!" blurted Allen. "We don't even know what's going on at the hospital! The police could be on their way to pick us up right now!"

"I don't hear any sirens," Terrence retorted.

"You'll hear them soon enough," Ron snapped back.

"So what are we supposed to do?" Terrence asked angrily. "Just walk into the hospital and stab Jay like we did Sandy?"

"We could suffocate him with a pillow," Allen suggested.

"Yeah right," said Terrence.

"Seriously, man, I say we sneak into his room when nobody's looking and take care of him," said Ron.

"And when will that be?" Terrence asked sarcastically.

"In the middle of the night," answered Ron.

The door to Ron's apartment opened, and his younger sister Stella peeped out. "Ron, Mama said come and eat!" she yelled.

"I've gotta go, guys, but I'll call you later," Ron said as he turned and hurried into the apartment before he got into trouble with Jimmy Lee.

Sadie Belle had checked every apartment, and no one had seen Joshua all day. Her neighbor, Jackie, sat in Sadie Belle's living room trying unsuccessfully to calm her down before her blood pressure got out of control. A tall, thin policeman named Dwight Quattleman also stood in her living room asking questions and writing answers on a small notepad.

"When did you last see your grandson, Ms. Brown?" Quattleman asked.

"He left the house around three o'clock and said he was going to play with his friend Marvin," Sadie Belle answered with a sniffle. "But Marvin says he ain't seen Joshua all day."

Quattleman scribbled on his notepad. "Do you know of anywhere else your grandson might have gone? Other friends or relatives? His parents?" he inquired with raised brows.

Sadie Belle told him she had checked every apartment in the complex. Quattleman kept writing.

"And none of them have seen him?" Quattleman asked rhetorically. "Do you remember what he was wearing when he left the house?"

"He had on a pair of cut-off blue jeans, but I can't remember what kinda shirt he was wearing," answered Sadie Belle. "I just didn't pay that much attention to what he had on. But I know he always wears them cut-off blue jeans."

"Do you have a recent picture of him?"

"I have his school pictures," said Sadie Belle pointing to a frameless picture that had been thumbtacked to the wall.

"Do you have a smaller one that I can take with me?" asked Quattleman.

"Yessir," answered Sadie Belle. "It's in my bedroom. I'll get it for you."

Sadie Belle retrieved a photo album from her bedroom and handed Quattleman a wallet-sized photo of Joshua. Quattleman took the photo and studied it for a moment.

"Is there any chance Joshua would run away, Ms. Brown?"

"Why in the world would he do something like that?" Sadie Belle asked with a serious frown.

Quattleman shrugged. "Sometimes kids do crazy things."

"My baby would never run away," Sadie Belle replied sternly.

"Where are Joshua's parents, Ms. Brown?" Quattleman asked.

"His mama lives in Chicago, but he wouldn't try to go there," Sadie Belle answered.

"What about his father?"

"You tell me," answered Sadie Belle.

"Does Joshua ever talk about wanting to be with his mother?"

"Look, Officer," interrupted Jackie, "Ms. Sadie Belle take good care of Joshua, and he very happy here with her."

"I just need to know these things," Quattleman responded. "These are just routine questions that I have to ask."

Quattleman studied his notepad momentarily as he searched for the right way to ask his next question. "Does Joshua have a birthmark or any other distinctive mark that would help us identify him, Ms. Brown?"

Sadie Belle's eyes widened. "Lord, have mercy!" she cried. "Do you think Joshua could be dead!"

"Oh, no!" Quattleman answered quickly. "I didn't mean to upset you, ma'am. This will just help us find him faster."

Sadie Belle took a deep breath. She couldn't bear to lose Joshua after all she'd been through with him. With his mother leaving him at birth, and his father no where to be heard of, Sadie Belle couldn't handle the thought of someone else having inflicted more pain upon her grandson.

"We'll do what we can to find your grandson, Ms. Brown," promised Quattleman. "As a matter of fact, he'll probably turn up any minute with some wild story to keep from getting a whuppin'."

"That's what I been tryin' to tell her myself," added Jackie.

"Thank you for your help, Officer Quattleman," said Sadie Belle.

# FOUR

The note attached to the refrigerator door read: "Gone to Karen's...be back around 5:30...Sandy." Larry Cassin was too tired to care where his daughter was that afternoon. His job as a supervisor over an assembly line at a warehouse always left him drained of any trace of energy by the end of the day, and he often wished he were still on the assembly line rather than bearing the mental turmoil of baby-sitting his crew all day. Nonetheless, working at the plant seemed to be his only option at the time. He had a mortgage to pay and a daughter to send to Catholic school – he could not let her down like her mother had.

Larry constantly blamed his wife for Sandy's rebellious behavior and the consequential trouble in which she often found herself. The strange boyfriends with more earrings than body parts to put them, the wild parties and the drinking, even Sandy's bout with bulimia were all his wife's fault. She had decided one day that being a wife and mother was no longer fulfilling. Larry suggested she go back to college and finish her degree, which is just what she did. But she decided that New York would be a much more exciting place to go to college than Mississippi. She never came back.

Larry had done all he could possibly think of to ease the hurt that Sandy showed, but nothing seemed to help. She continued to rebel and act out her pain. Although Larry put Sandy in parochial school to get her away from the bad crowd she hung around, she quickly found another. He had nearly wiped out his life's savings on counselors, with no results. Sandy was out of his control.

Larry turned on the TV and lay on the couch to catch the six o'clock news. Dinnertime at the Cassin house was not much of a family event. It was a grab-what-you-can-find-and-eat event. Larry had grabbed a couple of bologna sandwiches, a box of Bugles, and a root beer. That would be dinner and entertainment for the night.

Maybe he would take Sandy away to another city, another state. Maybe a change in scenery was what they both needed. Maybe even a new mother. Maybe it was time he actually spent quality time with her rather than sending her to counselors and Catholic schools, hoping other people could solve his problems. Maybe things could work out for them someday, he thought as he watched the motion on the television without hearing a sound.

---

Alone for the first time since his horrid adventure in the woods, Allen finally burst into tears. He lay across the bottom bunk of the beds he shared with his eight-year-old brother Timmy and buried his head in the flat pillow. He wanted out, but there was no way out. He was in trouble and he could be headed straight back to detention or jail.

He thought about his little brother who would have to face life without the help of a big brother to show him the ropes – not that he was much of an example for him anyway. But at least he could help him out if anybody tried to beat him up or bully him.

Allen's father had been killed in a car accident when Allen was ten and had left the family destitute. He had had no life insurance, and the little money the family received from his job barely covered the funeral costs. Allen's mother could hardly keep food on the table with the meager wages she made as a cashier, and to add to her burden, her aging father had moved in with them.

Allen heard heavy footsteps approaching his bedroom and he knew it was his grandfather, who wore heavy boots even in the middle of summer. As usual the old man opened the door without knocking and poked his head through. "Allen, there's someone here to see you," he said in a tired voice. "It's a colored boy, so I didn't let him in."

Allen quickly wiped his face on the pillow and sprang from the bed. "Chill out, Gramps, it's just Terrence," he said.

"You know, boy, in my day we didn't play with colored boys after we turned nine. You're too big to be fooling around with that boy."

Allen laughed. "Things have changed, Gramps. Jim Crow is dead."

The old man grunted. He failed to see the humor in Allen's comments.

Allen shook his head sympathetically and left his grandfather standing in the doorway.

"What's the plan?" he asked Terrence as he stepped out of the doorway.

"You didn't talk to Ron?" asked Terrence.

Allen shook his head.

"I got him to change his mind about Jay," said Terrence.

"What! What are we supposed to do now!" Allen cried.

"We've got a better plan," Terrence answered, trying to sound convincing.

"Ah, man!"

"No, listen, dude," pleaded Terrence. "All we have to do is bury the bodies in a good place. So if Jay starts talking about what happened, there won't be any bodies out there to prove what he's saying."

"And how are we supposed to bury the bodies?" Allen asked angrily.

"With a shovel."

"And where are we supposed to get a shovel?"

"From the old lady who lives in the last apartment on Manning."

"The one who's always sweeping the sidewalk?"

"Yup."

"So are you thinking of asking to borrow it or something?" Allen asked sarcastically.

"She never takes it in the house. We can borrow it without asking," answered Terrence.

"You mean steal it."

"Call it what you want."

Allen shut his eyes and leaned against the wall. Just when he thought things couldn't get any worse; he plots to steal from an old lady. "So what's the plan?" he asked solemnly.

"Can you sneak out tonight?" asked Terrence.

Allen nodded.

"Good. Midnight should be a good time."

"Midnight!"

"What? Did you think we were going out in the middle of the day?"

Allen rolled his eyes. "Okay, whatever," he grumbled.

"We'll meet at the playground, stop by the old lady's to pick up the shovel, then head to the woods."

"Man, I don't know if I can do this," Allen said shaking his head.

"You want to go to jail? Again?"

"Nope."

"Then you'll do it."

———

Rita finally took a break from Jay's bedside and went out for something to eat. The cafeteria was closed, so she had to go two blocks away to a burger joint. Her mother, Anna Koch, now sat in the stiff blue chair beside Jay's bed. Anna Koch was a petite woman just like her daughter. She too had auburn hair, yet at sixty, she had a little more gray than Rita.

Anna Koch was also a bitter woman – bitter at Rita for marrying at sixteen, bitter at Rita's ex-husband for leaving Rita with three hungry mouths to feed, bitter at her two grandsons for bringing shame to the family, bitter at her husband for dying of a heart attack at age fifty, and bitter at herself for not being able to find another man.

Now she was angry with the nurse for not bringing her a more comfortable chair. The chair in the room was hard and straight, and Anna was not accustomed to such simplicity – at least not since her husband died. Her plush home was elegantly furnished with Italian imports, and it was kept meticulously clean by a live-in maid. Her husband's death had left her with enough insurance money to live luxuriously for the rest of her days, and that was exactly what she was doing while her daughter and grandsons struggled to stay just beneath the poverty line.

It wasn't her fault, Anna always claimed. It was not her responsibility to financially support her daughter after she had reached adulthood. It was Rita's responsibility to deal with her own finances. Anna would offer moral support, but nothing else.

A nurse finally entered the room to check on Jay, and Anna grabbed the opportunity to ask for a better chair.

"Hi, I'm Bailey," she greeted. "I'll be Jay's nurse for this evening."

"May I have another chair. This one is so hard," Anna responded.

"Sure, I'll get you one," answered Bailey as she checked Jay's vital signs and IV "He's looking good," she commented to Anna.

"Poor thing," said Anna. "You know if his mama spent more time with him, he wouldn't be in this hospital. Two of my grandsons are already in jail for selling drugs. Can you believe it?"

Bailey smiled without a reply.

"I swear, I just don't know what to say about Rita," Anna continued. "She was such a sweet girl growing up until she hooked up with that no good Bubba Stringer."

Bailey tried to keep a straight face.

"Then she went and got knocked up in the back of his pickup truck. She thought I didn't know what she was doing, but time will always tell the truth of the matter."

"I'll go get that chair for you," Bailey said as she headed toward the door.

Anna caught her by the elbow. "Then she ran off and married Bubba. Sent her poor daddy straight to his grave. Then she went on to have three boys with Bubba. Two of 'em are in jail right now. They're just like Bubba – up to no good. But Jay'll be all right if his mama would just take care of him."

"I really need to go," Bailey tried again.

"And would you believe that after Rita had all them babies, that no good Bubba left her for another woman. Just left her with no job, no money, no food, nothing. And she's too scared to ask him to pay child support."

This was one time Bailey didn't care whether she appeared rude or not. She had to finish making her rounds and didn't want to stand there all night listening to Anna Koch downgrade her daughter to nothing. "I've got to go, ma'am," she said as she rushed from the room.

"Don't forget the chair, sweetie!" Anna yelled after her.

# FIVE

The refrigerator was practically empty as usual. Its contents included an old milk jug now filled with cold water, an empty mayonnaise jar, two eggs, three hotdogs, and two Old Milwaukee's. Terrence grabbed the three hotdogs and threw them into a pot of water. They would suffice for dinner.

He put the pot on the stove and went back into the living room. He let his body drop onto the dirty floral sofa and tried to relax his head unto a thinly cushioned pillow. There was no television to turn on, so Terrence just closed his eyes and relaxed while his hotdogs boiled.

Jesse, the man with whom Terrence lived, was not home yet. Terrence was glad. Frankly speaking, Jesse was a bum. He had no job, and he hung out in bars all day and drank. But he was all Terrence had at the time. Terrence felt as if he owed Jesse.

When Terrence was seven, his parents joined a crazy cult that convinced them that having children was evil. His parents believed it, abandoned Terrence, and ran off to Texas with the rest of the cult members.

A month after the McGees ran off and left their son, Jesse, who at the time had a real job as a truant officer, was scheduled to go out to the McGee home to find out why Terrence wasn't in school. He discovered that Terrence had been living alone for an entire month and was down to his last morsels of food. Jesse took Terrence to the Department of Family Services where they later discovered that Terrence would have to go to a group home because he had no relatives who would take him. They were all afraid of his parents' cult.

Feeling sorry for the poor kid, Jesse decided to take him in as a foster child. Things went well for the two for a while until alcohol got the best of Jesse. Now the two lived off Terrence's foster care check, food stamps, and any money Jesse could get from his lady friends.

Terrence got up to get his hotdogs and hoped there would be bread to go with them. He looked in the cabinet for a plate, but they were all dirty. He took a dirty one from the sink and rinsed it with hot water, then he searched for some bread. He found two slices, one being the dreaded end piece. Terrence took his three hotdogs, his two slices of bread, and a glass of water and sat down at the table to eat.

His meal seemed to disappear, leaving him just as hungry as when he started. He looked down at his Nike's and thought about selling them. But he wasn't that hungry. He had only a few more days before the food stamps would come in the mail. If he got to them before Jesse, maybe he could actually buy food before Jesse traded them for beer money.

Terrence hated his life and the people in it. He hated Jesse for being a drunk. He hated his parents for being fools. He hated the cult for being deceivers. He hated himself for being bad. Terrence dropped his head on the table and began to sob quietly. It was all he knew to do.

# SIX

Larry Cassin awoke and stared blankly at the noisy television screen. He couldn't believe he had slept so long. He didn't even hear Sandy come in. The house was pitch except for the light coming from the TV. Sandy usually kept the light over the stove on at night, but even it was off. Larry reached over and turned on a lamp. He looked at his watch and saw that it was a few minutes past midnight. He got up from the couch and made his way to the kitchen.

He was surprised to see that there was no evidence that Sandy had been in the kitchen to fix herself dinner. He wondered what time she had gotten home and why she hadn't awakened him. She hadn't even removed her note from the refrigerator door. Larry thought he'd better check on her.

Larry froze when he looked into his daughter's room and found it empty. He rushed back into the kitchen and snatched the note off the refrigerator door. He racked his brains trying to remember Karen's last name. "Davenport!" he yelled after his memory kicked in. He grabbed the phone book from the junk drawer and with shaking fingers flipped through to find the listings for Davenport. Luckily there was only one. Larry hastily dialed the number. After four rings there was a disgruntled, "Hello."

"This is Larry Cassin. Is my daughter still at your house?" he asked anxiously.

"What?" grunted the male voice on the other end.

Larry repeated his question, and the man on the other end hung up without answering. Larry pressed redial.

"Is this Karen Davenport's house?" he quickly asked after hearing a grumpy "Yeah?" from the other end.

"Who the devil wants to know?" asked the angry voice.

"This is Larry Cassin. I'm trying to find my daughter Sandy," Larry answered quickly before he got another dial tone.

"Do you realize what time it is?" grunted the man. "It's after midnight, buddy."

"I'm sorry for calling you at this hour, sir," Larry answered. "But my daughter left a note saying she would be at Karen's until five thirty, and she's not home yet."

There was a pause at the other end. "Well, I don't think Karen's had any company tonight," the man finally said.

"Not at all?" asked Larry.

"Nope."

Larry wasn't satisfied with the answer. "Do you mind if I speak to Karen?" he asked.

"As a matter of fact, I do."

"Look, Mr. Davenport, it's midnight, and I have no idea where my daughter is. You have a daughter, and you would be doing the same thing if she wasn't home right now."

Mr. Davenport hesitated for a moment. "Okay I'll let you speak to her," he said.

Karen came to the phone momentarily, but to Larry's chagrin she hadn't seen Sandy all week. Larry hung up and called the police.

---

An excruciating pain shot through his head as if his skull had been cracked, and the rest of his body responded by throbbing in agony as well. He managed to open his weary eyes only to observe the tiny soft lights produced by fireflies darting back and forth in the shadowy darkness of the night. An owl hooted in the distance, the moon cast a serene glow among the trees, and Joshua Tanner realized he was lying helplessly in the woods.

He rubbed his hand across his face and felt the dried blood on his mouth. Where did the blood come from, he wondered. His tiny body was racked with pain as he tried to get up. He managed to raise his torso from the hard ground. He looked around him observing the trees and wondering what he was doing lying among nature.

The owl hooted again, and Joshua knew he had to get up and go. But he had no idea where. He managed to get up, but he could hardly stand because of the pain in his head. The world around him was spinning, and he fell to his hands and knees and began to crawl blindly through the woods without the slightest idea where he was headed.

Joshua was petrified as he trekked swiftly through the brush, allowing twigs and sticks to poke him in his palms and bare knees. He was breathing heavily and tears streamed down his face. Suddenly his hand stumbled upon an unfamiliar object, which caused his elbow to crumble and sent Joshua crashing toward the ground. His fall was cushioned by the lifeless corpse of Sandy Cassin.

Joshua let out a scream that echoed throughout the woods. He quickly stumbled to his feet, ignoring the pain that he had felt before. He continued to scream as he stared at the bloodstained body of the dead girl. He began to run wildly through the woods, once again forgetting the agonizing pain in his head. He just wanted to get away from the dead body.

---

The moonlight danced among the trees as crickets played their songs and three tense teenagers roamed through the woods to accomplish their unthinkable mission. Ron gripped the flashlight as he led the pack to the spot where he and Jay had placed the bodies.

"I could've sworn we put Joshua here," Ron whispered nervously, shining the flashlight toward the spot where Joshua once lay.

"Well let's keep moving," said Terrence. "We don't have all night. He's out here somewhere. And stop that whispering. It's getting on my nerve."

Ron looked at the spot again. He was certain that it was where they had left the body. Confused, he led his friends through a few more weeds.

"See! I told you this was the spot!" Ron whispered excitedly, as he shined the flashlight toward Sandy's body.

"Okay," said Allen, suddenly feeling faint. "You don't have to shine the light on her for Pete's sake."

Ron slowly turned in a circle, scanning a small perimeter of the area near Sandy's body.

"Give me that!" yelled an irritated Terrence as he snatched the flashlight from Ron's hand. He walked a few feet, scanning the area intently. Ron used the light of the moon to see his way back to the spot where he was sure they'd left Joshua.

"Terrence! Allen!" Ron yelled.

"You found him?" asked Allen as he and Terrence rushed towards Ron.

"No. But I found this," Ron answered, holding up a green and red yo-yo.

"You found a yo-yo," Terrence sneered. "You called us over here to show us a stupid yo-yo."

"This yo-yo is proof that this is where we left Joshua," answered Ron.

"That yo-yo could belong to anybody," said Allen.

"It's Joshua's," Ron retorted.

"So do you think the body just got up and walked away, Ron?" Terrence asked rhetorically.

Ron kept his eyes fixed on the yo-yo, ignoring Terrence. He was certain that he had the right spot. He felt a sinking feeling in his stomach.

"Come on, guys. That body is around here somewhere, okay?" Allen said nervously. "It's just a stupid yo-yo that some kid left out here."

Ron clutched the yo-yo in his trembling hand. He knew to whom the yo-yo belonged.

"Let's quit playing games," said Terrence, who was quite furious at this point.

"I'm not playing games!" yelled Ron. "This is where we left Joshua, and he's not here anymore!" he said, almost sobbing.

"Then where is he?" asked Terrence.

"I don't know."

"This is ridiculous," said Terrence. "Let's just find the body. It didn't get up and walk away, you know."

"I'm telling you, he's gone!" cried Ron.

"Man, this is too weird," said Allen. "Let's just leave."

"You crazy!" Terrence screamed. "We came out here to bury some bodies, and we ain't leaving till we do!" he yelled angrily.

"Well you can just bury them by yourself 'cus I'm outta here!" cried Allen. "This place is too spooky for me. Dead bodies don't just get up and walk away."

"You sissy!" yelled Terrence. "Ron, get the shovel from him."

"You get it yourself. I'm outta here too," said Ron.

Terrence snatched the shovel from Allen. "Both of you are sorry," he said angrily. "I'll do it myself. I hope you can find your way back without a flashlight."

Ron and Allen left, and Terrence stood alone with the flashlight in one hand and the shovel in the other. He walked over to the spot where Ron claimed they'd left Joshua's body. He shined the light on the ground and noticed what appeared to be blood. He suddenly felt as if he were being watched. He dropped the shovel and ran.

"Hey! Wait up!" Terrence yelled as he stormed through the woods. "Hey, man," Terrence said, breathing heavily. "At first I thought you were lying, but I think I saw blood on the ground."

"This is crazy," said Allen.

The three boys walked quickly among the trees. Ron had begun to sweat profusely and his stomach knotted. He was sure that Joshua was dead when they'd left him. He held on tightly to the yo-yo, wishing he had left it behind.

"Do you think somebody found him?" asked Allen.

"Why would anybody take a dead body, man?" asked Terrence.

"Maybe he's not dead," said Ron.

"What d'ya mean 'Maybe he's not dead?'" asked Allen. "Didn't you guys check his pulse or anything?"

Ron shook his head.

"Stupid!" yelled Terrence.

"Hey! Back off, man!" Ron yelled back. "We're all in this together. Why didn't one of you guys make sure he was dead?"

"What if he's gone home?" asked Allen, his voice shaking.

"Have the police been by to see you?" asked Terrence.

"No."

"Then he hasn't gone home, has he?"

"What about the girl?" Allen asked.

"What about her?" replied Terrence.

"How do we know she's dead?"

"Duh!"

"What are we gonna do now?" asked Allen, his voice shaking.

"Nothing," answered Terrence.

"What about Joshua?" asked Ron.

"What about him?" asked Terrence.

"He's not out here. That's what."

"He's out here. And he's dead. You're just too stupid to remember where you put him," snapped Terrence.

"But what if he's not really dead?" asked Allen.

"Then we'll have to shut him up the right way this time," Terrence said angrily.

"What about Sandy? Aren't we gonna bury her?" asked Ron.

Terrence froze. "I left the shovel," he said. "We've gotta go back and get it."

"We?" asked Allen. "Not me. I'm going home."

"Ah, come on, dudes," Terrence pleaded. "I can't do this by myself. Besides all of our lives are on the line, even Jay's."

"No way, man," replied Ron. "I've gotta get home. If my dad finds those pillows under my sheets, he'll kill me."

"Then just imagine what he'll do when he finds out you stole a shovel to bury the people you killed today," Terrence said sharply.

Ron sighed hopelessly. "Okay, I'll go back with you."

"You with us, man?" Terrence asked Allen.

"One for all and all for one," Allen responded in despair.

# SEVEN

Detective C. E. Briggs, Jr. could feel his eyes swelling with tears as he tried to suppress a yawn that was desperate to get out. It was well past midnight, and he couldn't wait to get home and go to bed. Another alleged missing child call, probably a runaway, he thought as he stood in the living room of Larry Cassin, listening to Larry go on and on about how his good daughter hung out with a bad crowd – a classic story.

"You say she left a note saying she would be at a friend's house?" Briggs confirmed as if he hadn't heard it right the first time.

"Yes," Larry replied. "But Karen said that she hadn't seen Sandy all week."

"Does your daughter have a boyfriend?"

"Well, kinda."

"Kinda?"

"She's dated a few guys."

"Any chance she might be with one of them?"

"I hope not."

"Can you give me any names, Mr. Cassin?" Briggs asked.

"Frankly, I haven't been keeping up with my daughter's social life," Larry answered embarrassingly.

Briggs scribbled something on his notepad then rubbed his tired eyes. Another yawn was coming, and he could feel his face exploding as he tried to hold it in. "What about her friend Karen? Would she know any of these guys?"

"Probably," Larry said with a shrug.

"What's Karen's last name?"

"Davenport, and her number is 555-5787."

Briggs scribbled down the number. He'd check with Karen the following morning if the girl wasn't home by then. He was sure she was just out having a good time and had overlooked her curfew. She would probably be sneaking in any minute now, and the dad would feel like a jerk for bothering him.

"Was your daughter into drugs, Mr. Cassin?" Briggs asked routinely.

"Uh, probably."

"Probably?"

"Okay, yes," Larry answered harshly.

"Alcohol?" asked Briggs.

Larry took a deep breath. "Yes," he replied.

Briggs kept writing. "Any chance your daughter might be pregnant?"

Larry folded his arms and closed his eyes for a moment. It was hard answering such questions about his little girl, who he realized was no longer so sweet and innocent. "I really don't know, Officer. I know my daughter hangs out with a lot of different guys, but I really can't tell you what she's been up to."

"I regret to say, Mr. Cassin, that your daughter fits the description of a runaway."

Larry's heart sank into his stomach. Runaway or not, he needed Sandy home that night. Talking with Briggs had made him realize just how little attention he had been giving her. He would make time for her, he promised himself.

———

Sadie Belle had gone to bed at midnight like her doctor had advised her, but she just lay there staring at Joshua's picture as she wept and prayed. Her blood pressure was high and she could feel her head spinning. She knew that she needed to calm herself or she'd end up in the hospital where she'd be no good for Joshua.

Jackie, her neighbor, had finally gone home to tend to her own children at eleven o'clock, and Sadie Belle was alone again for the first time since she'd walked around the neighborhood looking for Joshua. She continued to stare at the photo and refused to believe that her grandson would run away. She was convinced that he was somewhere hurt. She just prayed that he wasn't dead.

The knock at the door startled Sadie Belle, and she instinctively jumped from the bed and grabbed her bathrobe just as she had always done when Joshua would scream in the middle of the night the first few weeks after his mother abandoned him. Sadie Belle hurried to the door. It had to be Joshua, she thought. Who else would be coming to her house so late?

She didn't bother asking, "Who is it?" like she'd always taught Joshua to do, she simply yanked the door open as fast as she could. There to greet her stood Jackie and her two children.

"I just wanted to check on you, Ms. Sadie Belle," she said. "I kept thinking about you, and I just couldn't sleep."

"I'm okay, Jackie," Sadie Belle replied, her heart broken when it wasn't Joshua who stood on the other side of the door. "You really don't need to stay with me. I'll be all right."

"You sure?"

"I'm sure."

"Okay, then," said Jackie. "You call me if you need me, Ms. Sadie Belle."

"Thank you, Jackie," Sadie Belle responded as she closed the door. She went back to bed and wept.

---

"Come on, dudes, we might as well bury this body while we're here," Terrence tried to convince his buddies as he picked up the shovel.

Ron and Allen looked at each other and shrugged. Terrence took it as a "yes" and stuck the shovel into the hard ground. Ron and Allen stood by as if on guard. Terrence ordered them to cover up the body with some brush from the woods while he dug the hole. That way they didn't have to look at it. Ron kept envisioning his father walking into his bedroom, discovering his absence. He would be better off in juvenile detention, at least they didn't give beatings with extension cords and wire clothes hangers.

"What's that?" Ron whispered nervously as he quickly tossed branches over the body so that he wouldn't need to be near it long.

"What's what?" asked Terrence, looking up from his digging.

"I heard something over there," Ron answered, pointing toward a cluster of trees.

Allen shined the flashlight toward the trees, revealing nothing. "Just your imagination playing tricks on you," he told Ron.

The noise came again, only loud enough for all ears to hear this time. All eyes fell toward the trees. Allen flashed the light into the darkness of the trees. All three boys screamed. A set of glowing red eyes peered out of the darkness. The predator made no sound but stared intently at its prey. The three boys ran as quickly as their legs could carry them, again leaving the shovel behind. The harmless deer stepped out of the darkness and continued to stare at the fleeing trio.

———————

Joe Hopkins pressed the scan button on the radio until he found an oldies station. He heard the voice of Stevie Wonder, but couldn't remember the name of the song. It was on the tip of his tongue, of course. "What's the name of that song?" he asked his wife Marsha.

Marsha listened to the words. "Oh, I can't remember either," she answered.

"I guess old age is getting the best of us," Joe said as he yawned. Then he noticed the sadness in his wife's eyes.

"I'm sorry. I shouldn't have said that," he apologized.

Marsha wiped a tear from her eye. "You're right," she told her husband. "I am getting old, and I might as well face it."

Marsha was forty-two and had just miscarried the baby that she had been trying to have for over fifteen years. Or at least that's what she had believed until her doctor confirmed she was never pregnant. For three months Marsha had experienced morning sickness, vomiting, weight gain, and every other hormonal change that came with pregnancy. Then something went wrong. Marsha's doctor had her come in for an ultrasound to determine whether there was a problem with the pregnancy. The results of the ultrasound mystified Marsha and Joe. No image appeared on the monitor. Marsha had experienced all the symptoms of pregnancy, but no baby had ever formed in her womb. The devastation had been too much for Marsha to handle, so Joe had taken her on a road trip to Canada for a vacation.

The highway was practically empty. It reminded Marsha of her egg supply. Marsha watched the road as carefully as Joe as he cruised along at 55 miles per hour. Joe was old-fashioned and had not yet adjusted to the 65-mile-per-hour speed limit.

Marsh saw the figure moving along the side of the road long before the car reached it. It looked like a person, but she couldn't be sure in the darkness.

"Slow down," she ordered her husband. Joe obeyed. Marsha leaned closer to the dashboard. "Do you see something up there moving along the side of the road?"

Joe leaned forward and strained his tired eyes. "Yeah. Probably a dog."

As the car got closer, the figure became clearer. "It looks like a person, Joe."

"It is a person!" Joe exclaimed. "My word, I think it's a child!"

Marsha felt the car decelerating. "What are you doing!" she exclaimed nervously.

"I'm stopping," Joe answered.

"No! This could be some kind of trick! Someone could be in those woods waiting!" Marsha cried.

"That's a chance we'll have to take," Joe answered. "That child might be hurt," he said as he eased his car onto the shoulder of the road.

"Joe, please don't stop the car," Marsha pleaded. She could see the tiny body almost jogging along the road. She felt sorry for him but didn't want to take any chances with her own life. Her husband reasoned differently.

Joe stopped the car and unbuckled his seatbelt. "I'll be right back," he said.

Marsha prayed as she watched her husband jog to catch up with the strange boy. She began to look around nervously, expecting someone to jump out of the woods with a gun and attack her husband. She unbuckled her seatbelt and crossed over to the driver's seat. She pressed 9-1-1 on her cell phone, but didn't press the call button. She would at least be ready to drive off and call 9-1-1 if she had to.

Fortunately Joe returned seconds later carrying a small boy in his arms. Marsha crossed back over to the passenger's side and hurriedly unlocked the doors for Joe. Joe placed the boy on the back seat and quickly jumped into the driver's seat. He sped off.

# EIGHT

When the boys thought they had put a safe distance between themselves and the mysterious eyes, they slowed down to catch their breath.

"Did you see that?" asked Ron nervously.

"Man, what was that thing?" responded Allen.

"We blew it!" Terrence cried angrily. He was no longer concerned about the eyes in the darkness, but about what their next plan would be. "We blew it," he repeated to himself.

"What are we gonna do now?" Allen asked as the three headed home. "What if Joshua goes back home?"

"Why are you always asking me questions!" Terrence snapped. "Don't you have a brain?"

Allen tried to ignore Terrence. He knew he was just irate over not getting the job done. He would forgive him for calling him stupid. He wouldn't add him to his hitlist of all the people who'd deflated his self-esteem. He realized they were all in the same boat now. The last eight hours had been a nightmare from which he couldn't wait to wake up.

"We need to hurry," Ron said. "I've got to get home."

"Yeah, me too," added Allen.

"Look, guys, I'm sorry," said Terrence. "I lost my cool. I didn't mean what I just said, Allen."

"No sweat, man," replied Allen.

"What about the old lady's shovel?" asked Ron.

"That's the least of our worries," Terrence answered.

The boys finally reached the end of the woods and stepped onto the dirt road that led to the back of the housing complex. All was dark and quiet. There were no police cruisers on the scene. The boys felt it was still safe to go home.

———

Everyone in the car was silent. Marsha Hopkins was still shaken by the terrifying experience on the highway. Joe was now driving a little faster than 55. And Joshua Tanner had no idea what was happening to him.

"What are we gonna do with him, Joe?" Marsha whispered nervously.

"We're taking him to a hospital," Joe answered. "He looks like he's been beaten."

"I don't need to go to the hospital," Joshua quickly interrupted. "I'm okay."

"What's your name, son?" Joe asked as he glanced at Joshua through the rearview mirror.

For the first time since he had awakened in the woods, Joshua suddenly realized that he couldn't remember his name. But he couldn't allow these strangers to know that, however. "Teddy," he quickly answered without thinking.

"What's your last name, Teddy?" Joe inquired.

"Uh," said Joshua as he stumbled for a last name. "Bear," he finally said.

"Teddy Bear?" Joe asked with raised brows as he glanced over at Marsha. "That's a strange name."

"Uh, that's just my nickname," Joshua answered quickly. "My real name is, uh, Michael."

"Michael?" repeated Joe.

"Yes, Michael. Michael Jord---, I mean Jones."

Joe and Marsha looked at each other. "What are you doing on the highway this late at night, Michael?" asked Joe.

Joshua looked down at his dirty clothes, and he thought about the blood on his face. What would he tell these people? He didn't know what he was doing on the highway. He thought about the dead girl and realized that something horrible had happened in the woods. For all he knew, he could have been a murderer. He couldn't tell these strangers the truth; they might take him to the police and have him put away for life. He had to think fast and think smart this time.

"My parents left me on the highway," he answered in a low, sad voice.

"What!" responded the Hopkins in unison.

"My dad stopped the car and beat me right there on the highway, then he got back in the car and drove off without me."

"That's horrible!" exclaimed Marsha. "Are you hurt badly?" she asked.

"My head hurts a little," Joshua answered. "And my chest," he added.

"We're finding a hospital right now," said Joe.

"Oh, I'm not hurt all that bad," Joshua chimed in swiftly. "I've had lots of whuppins before."

"We're taking you to the hospital anyway and calling the police," Joe said.

Marsha took out her cell phone again.

"No!" screamed Joshua.

"What!" Joe and Marsha cried back in disbelief.

"You can't do that," pleaded Joshua. He had to think of another lie quickly and he knew it had to be a good one. "You can't call the police on my daddy. The rest of the family needs him cause my mama can't work."

"He's a child abuser," Joe responded unemotionally.

"I'm the only one he beats," Joshua answered. "He don't hit the other six kids."

Joe and Marsha looked at each other again. Marsha held on to the phone.

"Why does he beat you?" Joe asked.

"Because I do bad things," Joshua answered in a babyish voice.

"Nothing could be bad enough to make your father leave you stranded on the highway," replied Joe.

"Oh, it's bad," lied Joshua. "Believe me, it's bad."

"What are we going to do?" Marsha asked Joe.

Joe shrugged. He had a dubious look on his face.

"I'm not lying. I swear," Joshua hurriedly interjected. "Can't you just take me home with you? Nobody will miss me."

"What about your mother?" Marsha asked.

"This is ridiculous!" Joe snapped. "We're taking you to the hospital and that's that."

"Nooo!" whined Joshua, thinking about the dead body in the woods and not knowing whether he was to blame. "He will beat Mommy!"

"Joe," Marsha interceded. "It's late. Can't we work this out in the morning?"

Joe shook his head.

"The boy is obviously scared to death of what his father might do," she said in a lowered voice. "He might try to run away from us if we try to take him to a hospital."

Joe sighed. "This is ludicrous, Marsha," he said shaking his head. "Who would leave a child on the highway?"

"People have done stranger things, Joe," Marsha answered.

Joe sighed again. "Okaaay," he said, "but first thing in the morning, we call the police."

Joshua finally breathed a breath of relief and smiled when he saw Marsha put away her cell phone.

Joe kept past the next exit. Now all Joshua had to do was keep his lies straight.

# NINE

Eight o'clock in the morning was a little early for basketball, but Terrence, Allen, and Ron pretended to play anyway. They had all made it back to their beds undetected the night before but could only wonder what the day held for them. They knew that Joshua was no longer in the woods, but whether or not he was with his grandmother was another story. Neither of them dared inquire about him. That would be as bad as turning themselves in.

They were also paranoid about what might be going on with Jay. Had he talked or was he still unconscious? Should they go ask about him or just wait for the cops to come pick them up? They knew that asking too many questions could lead to suspicion.

"Man, I wish I could just disappear!" Ron screamed as he slammed the basketball into the backboard.

"I think we should just turn ourselves in," Allen said meekly. "There's no way we're getting away with this now that that kid's on the loose."

Terrence picked up the discarded basketball and began dribbling methodically. He was silent as he stared in the direction of the woods. He was sweating not only from the ninety-degree morning heat but also from his feeling of despair and desperation. Why did Jay even have to get involved with the likes of Sandy Cassin? He knew that she was always up to no good when she came prancing around the projects. She had already landed Darrell and Stephen a jail sentence.

Terrence's thoughts were abruptly interrupted by the sound of a horn. He turned toward the direction of the street and saw Rita Stringer's Ford Escort. She had spent the night at the hospital and was on her way home to get dressed for work. She pulled to the side and motioned for the boys to come to the car. She looked as if she could be smiling from what the boys could tell.

Terrence was the first to cautiously approach the car. "Hey, Ms. Rita," he said with a wave of his hand. "How's Jay?"

"Much better than yesterday," Rita replied. Her eyes were red from lack of sleep, but they still had sort of a sparkle of relief. "I guess he just needed a good night's sleep. He just woke up this morning like nothing had happened yesterday," Rita said shrugging her shoulders.

"He's awake?" Allen asked without holding back the panic in his throat. Terrence elbowed him, warning him to be careful.

"Yes," Rita answered. "The doctor thinks he might be able to come home later today."

"Did he ask about us?" Terrence inquired, being careful not to arouse suspicion with his words.

"He did," answered Rita with a nod. "That's why I was glad to see ya'll out here."

Terrence braced himself. Ron started sweating. Allen bit a fingernail.

"He told me to ask you about a package you were holding for him," said Rita.

"A package?" Terrence repeated, trying not to let his voice choke.

"Yeah," answered Rita, her eyebrows furrowed. "He wanted to make sure you still had it."

"I'm not sure I know what he's talking about," Terrence answered. He was lying.

"Well he sure did seem to be worried about it," replied Rita. "That's the first thing he mentioned when he woke up. You sure he didn't give you anything yesterday?"

Terrence shrugged. "Not that I can remember," he said glancing at Ron and Allen reminding them not to say anything.

"He didn't give any of you anything?" Rita asked.

Allen and Ron shook their heads.

"Okay," said Rita. "Maybe he was still a little shaken from yesterday and didn't know what he was talking about."

"Musta been," said Terrence.

"I've gotta go get ready for work," said Rita. "I won't be able to pick up Jay until this evening. You can talk to him them cause he sure seemed worried about this package."

Terrence nodded. Rita waved and drove off.

Terrence felt as if he'd been stabbed in the stomach. Jay was once again messing things up.

———————

"How could Jay be soooo stupid," Allen said shaking his head. His voice was calm for a change. "I can't believe he would say something about the package to his mama."

"I wonder if anybody's at the hospital with him," Ron said with a sinister look on his face. "We should just go shut that fool up right now."

"The only person who needs to be shut up is you," said Terrence. "We'll all be locked up soon enough anyway."

"Why do we all have to go to jail?" asked Allen. "Ron and Jay are the ones who committed the crimes."

Before Allen knew what was going on, Ron had grabbed him by the neck and started choking him. Terrence pulled him back.

"Dude, are you crazy!" he yelled at Ron.

"Man, he's talking about turning me in!" he yelled at Terrence. "You think I'm just gon' stand here and let him do that?"

Terrence held on to Ron. Allen rubbed his neck. He was scared of what might happen if Terrence let go of Ron.

"Nobody's tellin' on anybody!" Terrence said sternly. "Allen, you were right there in the woods when this all happened. That makes you just as guilty."

Allen was afraid to say anything, but his thoughts were on how he could get a lighter judgment. That's how it always happened on TV. Why should he have to spend all that time in jail when all he did was watch?

# *TEN*

Joshua devoured the bacon and pancakes Marsha had prepared for him. He had slept late that morning, and the hunger pains in his stomach had become violent. Joe had gotten up earlier and was already out running errands. Joshua didn't mind. The more he stayed away from him, the fewer lies he would have to tell. Besides, Marsha was the one Joshua felt he could trust. Joe would turn him in to the cops in a heartbeat.

Joshua took a moment to look up from his bacon to admire the Hopkins' kitchen. Everything about it was perfect, just like in a magazine, Joshua thought. Shucks, the whole house was perfect, Joshua thought. Marsha included. She would be just right for a mommy. She was nice and pretty. She let him sleep late and made him breakfast. They even had fresh orange juice. Marsha had even made Joe go to the store early that morning and buy breakfast items just for Joshua. Joshua could live there forever.

"I can't imagine why anyone would leave a child stranded on the highway," Marsha said for the third time as she unloaded the dishwasher.

"I bet people probably do it all the time," Joshua said with a shrug as he glanced down at his clothes that Marsha had washed and dried before he got up.

"Not normal people," said Marsha.

"My daddy's normal," said Joshua. "He's a cook."

"You mean he should be cooked," Marsha said heatedly.

"Ah, he ain't that bad," said Joshua. "I just stayed in trouble all the time, and he couldn't handle it."

Marsha frowned. "What kind of trouble could a little boy like yourself get into?"

"You don't wanna know," Joshua said with a wave of his hand. He thought about the body in the woods. He had to wonder himself what kind of kid he was. And what was his daddy really like? He was having a very hard time remembering anything about himself.

"I'd like to know more about you, Michael," Marsha said as she strolled over to the table and sat across from Joshua.

Joshua shrunk back. She was going to ask too many questions, he thought. She was going to find him out while her husband was gone. That was the plot, Joshua was sure. She appeared to be nice, feed him, wash his clothes, butter him up, then get him to talk.

"Do you have any children?" Joshua quickly asked, trying to divert the attention from himself.

"Nope," answered Marsha, and for the first time she didn't feel sad about it.

"Why not?" Joshua prodded on.

"Oh, I don't know," sighed Marsha. "Just too busy I guess. But enough about me. I want to know more about you," she said.

Joshua felt a tingle go up his spine. "I'm just a regular kid living a regular life," he said with a nervous laugh. "Not a whole lot to tell you. By the way, where's Mr. Joe?"

"Out washing the car," Marsha answered. "That's what he always does when we come back from a trip," she said, smiling softly at Joshua. He would make a perfect son, she reasoned. Maybe this was fate. He had been abandoned, and she couldn't have any children. It all fit perfectly.

"You go on trips a lot?" Joshua asked.

"Quite a bit," Marsha answered.

"Ever been to Atlanta?" asked Joshua.

Marsha nodded. "Many times," she said.

"I wanna go there to Six Flags," Joshua said with a glow on his face.

"Maybe your parents will take you there one day," Marsha said, trying to prod more information from him.

"I don't plan to ever go back home," Joshua replied. "I thought maybe I could just stay here with you seeing that you don't have any children or nothing."

Marsha chuckled slightly. "You know, I'm glad we found you. We could use someone around here to walk the dog," she added.

"You have a dog!" Joshua beamed.

Marsha smiled and nodded.

"Where? What kind?"

"He's at my friend's house. That's where he stays when we're out of town."

"What kind is he? What's his name?" Joshua asked excitedly.

"Calm down," Marsha said laughing. "He's a black lab, and his name is Max."

"Ah, man, this is awesome. A dog," Joshua said.

"Joe will pick him up on his way home from the carwash."

"Cool!" Now Joshua knew he never wanted to leave.

———————

News had spread throughout the Roseville Housing Project that little Joshua Tanner was missing. Now several of Joshua's neighbors along with a couple of police officers were headed to the woods behind the housing project to look for him. The children were known to wander into the woods despite numerous warnings against it. In addition, Joshua's friend Marvin had finally confessed to Joshua's plan of sneaking into the woods on the previous afternoon.

The search had not begun until around 3 P.M. the day after Joshua's disappearance. Sadie Belle had chosen to stay home. She couldn't bear the thought of walking upon Joshua's body in the woods. Several teenagers had joined in the search with the two policemen and their dog. Terrence,

Ron, and Allen, needless to say, were not among them. They all pretended they had more important things to do.

One of the policemen on the search was, of course, Dwight Quattleman, who was more than anxious to find Joshua especially since this was his first case. He also felt sorry for Sadie Belle, who by now was at the point of a nervous breakdown. When he had stopped by the apartment to ask for any of Joshua's personal items for the dog to sniff, he noticed that everything in the apartment was just as it was the day before. The food that Sadie Belle had been preparing for dinner sat on the stove untouched. Her hair was uncombed and she was still wearing the same clothes from the previous day. Even Quattleman couldn't bear the thought of having to tell her the news if they found Joshua's body.

The search party had spread out, but the policemen stayed with the dog. The dog led them straight in the direction of the pond.

"I hope he hasn't drowned," Quattleman said pointing toward the pond.

"You know every kid thinks he can swim cause they can do it in the bathtub," commented the other policeman.

At that moment the dog began to run toward the pond. The two policemen followed. Quattleman felt a rush of panic sweep through his body. He was sure the dog had found Joshua. The dog sniffed wildly around the pond. Quattleman noticed there was blood in the spot that had the dog's attention.

"What we got here, boy?" he addressed the dog as he knelt to observe the spot. "Hey, take a look at this," he said to the other policeman as he picked up a bloodstained leaf.

The other policeman observed the leaf then carefully placed it in an evidence bag. The dog continued sniffing out Joshua's trail then suddenly ran toward a pile of branches and dead leaves.

"Hey, looks like we've found something!" Quattelman yelled as he ran after the dog. The other policeman followed.

Quattleman stopped cold in his tracks. He stared with his mouth agape at the eyesore that lay before him. Under the brush lay the body of Sandy Cassin. Dried blood covered her yellow tank top.

# ELEVEN

It was 7:30 P. M. The sun was disappearing from the sky as Detective Briggs reluctantly rang the doorbell of the Cassin home. He had been a detective in New York for several years, so he had performed this horrid task several times before. It had not gotten any easier. He stood at the door of the white-brick ranch home, which was nestled among trees that lined a quiet street in a blue-collar suburban neighborhood, and wondered how a girl from such a nice neighborhood would wound up dead in a neck of woods behind a housing project.

Larry opened the door only seconds after the doorbell rang. His unshaven face looked sad and worn. He was still wearing yesterday's clothes. He had not bothered going to work or calling in.

"Good evening, Mr. Cassin," Briggs said as nonchalantly as possible.

Larry responded with a stare. He had spent the entire day investigating his daughter's whereabouts. He had talked to neighbors, all of Sandy's friends that he knew of, relatives, and friends of the family. He had even tracked down his wife in New York, just in case Sandy had gone there.

"I think we might have found your daughter," Briggs said sympathetically.

Larry's heart sank.

"We can't be sure," Briggs said with hesitation. "We can't be sure until the body has been identified."

Larry's legs grew weak and he grabbed the doorknob to keep from falling. He opened his mouth to speak, but nothing came out. Briggs stared at him pitifully. "I'm sorry," was all he knew to say.

---

Quattleman felt a mixture of hope and disappointment when Joshua's body wasn't found in the woods. He was hopeful that Joshua was still alive, yet he was disappointed that he knew of nowhere else to look. He and Joshua's neighbors had remained in the woods until past sunset. The dog had led them to the highway and back without a trace of Joshua except a yo-yo that was found near the edge of the woods. Marvin had later identified it as Joshua's.

"Hey, Quattleman," he heard someone call him from behind as he retrieved his chips from the vending machine. Quattleman turned toward the door of the break room and returned the greeting to Detective Briggs.

"It's late. You should've been gone hours ago," said Briggs.

Quattleman shrugged. "Thought I'd join you on the graveyard shift."

"Seriously, what are you doing here so late, man?"

"I've got a lot of catching up to do, plus I really need to find that kid, Joshua Tanner. His grandmother is so worried that she might end up in the hospital."

Briggs shook his head. "It's a shame, man, that people could be so sick and hurt children. Look what somebody did to the Cassin girl."

"That's what we're afraid of," replied Quattleman. "You know we found evidence that Joshua Tanner had been in those woods, don't you?"

Briggs nodded.

"The dog sniffed his trail all the way to the highway," said Quattleman.

"You think he knows anything about the Cassin murder?"

"It's likely."

"How do you know he wasn't just out there and left before the murder happened?"

"We've matched his bloodtype to blood found at the scene," answered Quattleman. "So we suspect it might be his."

"Scary," Briggs said with a cringed forehead. "You think he was kidnapped?"

"Maybe," answered Quattleman.

"But why?" asked Briggs. "What would anybody have to gain by holding on to a poor kid from the projects?"

"Definitely not ransom," said Quattleman.

"Maybe they took him and dropped him off somewhere. That's possible, isn't it?" Briggs asked, trying to instill hope into his friend.

Quattleman laughed nervously. "Yeah, right," he said. "All we can do is start posting his picture everywhere and hope that someone has seen him."

"I just hope he isn't dead," said Briggs. "One murder in this community has been too much already."

Quattleman crunched on a chip and took a gulp of soda. The last thing he wanted to do was tell Sadie Belle Brown that her grandson was dead. He knew they would have to bury her too.

# TWELVE

Joe Hopkins figured he had given his wife plenty of time to think about what they would do with Michael. Marsha was a sensible woman, he thought, at least sensible enough to realize that they could go to jail for kidnapping if they didn't report this child to the proper authorities. Indeed he felt sorry for her. She had grown quite attached and was acting as if nothing strange had happened in the last twenty-four hours. But Joe knew they had to do the right thing.

Joe stepped out of his office where he was preparing lectures for his summer school class that would be starting in a few weeks. He found Marsha and Joshua sitting in the den. Joshua was playing with the new PlayStation game that Marsha had bought him earlier that day, and Marsha sat on the sofa watching him with delight. Joshua was clad in a pair of new khaki shorts and a blue and white Jackson State Tigers T-shirt. Marsha had taken him shopping and practically bought him an entire wardrobe in one day.

The two looked picture-perfect together, Joe thought. Maybe this was how they would be finally blessed with a child of their own, he reasoned, then shook the thought from his head. He was thinking as irrationally as Marsha. If they were going to keep the child, they would still have to do it legally.

"What's up, little man?" Joe asked Joshua as he knelt on the floor beside him.

"Just playing Crash Bandicoot," Joshua answered without missing a beat on the game.

"Looks like you're pretty good at it," said Joe. "Where'd you learn to play."

Joshua shrugged his shoulders as he leaned sideways to keep up with the game.

"You play at home?" asked Joe.

"Uh, yeah," Joshua responded distractedly.

"What else do you like to do at home?" Joe continued.

Joshua lost his concentration and consequently the game. He wished Joe would leave him alone and stop asking so many questions. Why couldn't he just be like Marsha and let him play with the dog and buy him things? "I like to play with my dog," Joshua answered as he looked over at Marsha who was smiling with approval.

"So you have a dog?"

Joshua nodded.

"Don't you miss him?" asked Joe.

"Nope. I can just play with yours. He's better'n mine anyway."

"Well don't you miss your mommy?" Joe tried again.

"Nope. And she don't miss me either," answered Joshua.

"How do you know that?" asked Joe.

"Cause she let my daddy drive off without me," Joshua answered with a feeling of satisfaction.

Joe gave up and let Joshua play his game. He sat beside Marsha on the sofa. They looked at each other and smiled. Joe could see joy in his wife's eyes for the first time in weeks. "We need to talk," he finally said. Marsha stopped smiling.

The two got up and went into Joe's office, leaving Joshua alone with the PlayStation. Joe closed the door to his office and walked over to the window where Marsha was standing. She was crying.

"Please don't cry," Joe pleaded.

Marsha walked angrily away from the window. She wiped away the tears with the back of her hand. "I know what you want," she said sternly. "And I say 'no'."

"Marsha, the police will know how to handle this," said Joe. "We have no choice."

"If we take him to the police, we may never see him again," Marsha said in a shaky voice.

"Listen to yourself, Marsha," Joe said firmly. "You're contemplating keeping a child that we found on the highway and not even notifying the police. It doesn't make any sense."

"I'm not losing another child!" Marsha screamed.

"He's not your child!" Joe yelled back. "He belongs to someone else, Marsha," he said in a lowered voice.

"They don't even want him," Marsha said angrily.

"That's for a judge to decide," said Joe. "This nonsense has gone on long enough."

"I won't let you do it," Marsha said defiantly.

Joe sighed. "We're taking him to the police, and that's final," he said bluntly.

"Over my dead body," Marsha said slowly as she turned and stormed from the room.

Joe picked up the phone and dialed the police.


Before Joe could speak a word, he quickly hung up the phone when he heard the sound of his car backing out of the driveway. Within seconds, Marsha had grabbed Joshua and fled. Joe hurried to the front door to try to stop them, but he was too late. Marsha was already down the street by the time he got outside. Joe rushed back inside to get his keys.

# THIRTEEN

Terrence had seen Rita Stringer's car pass by earlier in the evening and had noticed that Jay was not with her. When he called to find out what had happened, Rita informed him that Jay had had a setback. He had broken out into sweats again and his temperature was up. The doctor didn't know why he would be displaying symptoms of shock again, but he wanted him to remain in the hospital for another day. The only explanation that Terrence could think of was that Jay had found out about the police finding Sandy Cassin's body and had freaked out again. This incident made him realize that Jay was as weak as Ron and Allen claimed him to be and probably a bigger threat than the missing Joshua Tanner.

Terrence heard a key turn in the lock, and he knew it was Jesse. Terrence had a feeling that Jesse was drunk because he'd left earlier with one of his drinking buddies, and he mentioned stopping by the pawnshop. Terrence knew he didn't want a confrontation with the drunken slob, so he leaped from the couch and headed to his room but didn't get there before Jesse entered the apartment.

"The thrill is gon'" Jesse sang out in a loud, obnoxious voice as he staggered through the doorway. "The thrill is gon' 'way," he continued, slamming the door behind him.

Terrence hurried into his room.

"Hey, boy!" Jesse yelled. "I need t' talk t' ya," he said, stumbling towards Terrence.

"I'm going to bed," Terrence answered without looking toward Jesse.

"Boy, don' walk 'way from me when I'm talkin!'" yelled Jesse, the stench of his alcohol-ridden breath filling the air.

Terrence tried to shut the door of his bedroom. Jesse followed him, kicking the door open.

"Get out of my room, Jesse," Terrence said calmly, remembering what had happened to the last person who had crossed Jesse while he was drunk.

"I needs some money," Jesse slurred, stumbling into the room.

"I don't have any," Terrence answered, trying to move away from the offensive odor.

"Don't lie t' me, boy," Jesse said. He had a wicked grin on his face.

"I'm not lying," answered Terrence. "You know I won't have any money until Tuesday, man, when the check comes."

Jesse leaned against the wall for support. "I ain't talkin' 'bout no check," he said as he began to laugh wickedly.

Terrence felt a nerve twitch under his eye. "I don't know what you're talking about," he said as he tried to keep his voice from shaking.

"Oh, you know," Jesse said while still laughing mockingly.

Terrence tried to force a blank look, but Jesse wasn't buying it.

"I seen the lil' stash you hidin' in yo' closet," Jesse said as he pointed toward Terrence's bed.

"You're just drunk and crazy, man," Terrence said nervously. "I don't have anything in my closet."

"You take me f' a fool, boy?" Jesse asked angrily.

"N-no, Sir," Terrence answered, trying not to increase Jesse's anger. "I don't take you for a fool."

"Don' mock me, boy," Jesse said in a low hoarse voice.

"I'm not mocking you, Jesse," Terrence said quietly. "I would just like to go to bed, please."

"You ain' doin' nothin' 'til you gi' me dat bag outta da closet," Jesse said as he moved toward the closet.

"Look, man, just get out of my room," Terrence pleaded. "I'll give you the whole check on Tuesday," he lied.

Jesse ignored him and proceeded toward the closet.

"Man, get out of my closet!" Terrence yelled.

Jesse continued to ignore him and started throwing clothes out of the closet. Terrence had had enough. He leaped toward Jesse and tried to pull him out of the closet. A vicious elbow sent him flying back toward the window. Without warning, Jesse was all over Terrence. Terrence threw the drunken slob onto the floor. He quickly got up and reached for one of his basketball trophies from his windowsill.

Jesse retaliated. He sprang from the floor and tackled Terrence, knocking him against the wall and the trophy to the floor. He swung a heavy fist into Terrence's stomach. Terrence crumbled to the floor. Jesse fell on top of him again and pinned him to the floor with his knees. With both hands he grabbed Terrence's neck and began choking him and banging his head against the thinly carpeted floor. Though barely able to breathe, Terrence managed to probe the floor for the trophy. He found it and swung it wildly into the air.

Jesse screamed and grabbed the side of his head, freeing his grip on Terrence's throat. Terrence tried to stand up but staggered back to the floor. He maintained his grip on the trophy, ready to strike again if necessary.

Jesse slumped to the floor and groaned loudly. Terrence saw blood gushing from Jesse's head. Jesse rolled over onto his back, and the groaning stopped. He was unconscious.

# FOURTEEN

Joe rushed to the garage only to find out that his gas tank was empty. Marsha had always warned him about not filling the tank. She had warned him that there would be an emergency one day and he wouldn't have gas in his car. He knew that Marsha had gotten too much of a lead on him to catch her, especially since he didn't know where she was going. He figured his best option was to call the police.

Joe rushed to the phone and dialed 9-1-1, but quickly hung up before the operator answered. What was he thinking? What would he tell the police? That his crazy wife ran off with a child they found on the highway? He reasoned that that would not be a good idea. Marsha would be accused of kidnapping, and Joe couldn't let that happen. Going out to look for them would probably be pointless. He decided to call his friend Officer Dennis Moorehouse directly. He would know how to handle the situation.

Joe and Dennis had been roommates in college, but Joe never thought he would need to talk to Dennis professionally. He had lived his entire life without having a run-in with the law, and now this. If only he had taken the boy straight to the police when they found him, Dennis wouldn't be standing in his living room dressed in a blue uniform.

"You know this is so unlike Marsha to do something so crazy," Joe said, trying very hard not to show too much emotion.

"Trust me, Joe," replied Dennis. "I'm finding it hard to believe that you two had a fight."

Joe fiddled his fingers. He had not yet mentioned Joshua.

"I still don't know why you called me," said Dennis. "I'm sure Marsha just left to let off some steam."

Joe took a deep breath. "There's more to it than that," he said, embarrassed.

"Oh," replied Dennis with a raised eyebrow.

"You see," Joe started as he shifted his feet a bit. "The fight didn't involve just the two of us. There's this little boy," said Joe as he stuffed his hands into his pockets and began to pace around the room. He still wasn't sure what to tell Dennis. He didn't know just how much trouble they might be in, especially Marsha.

"What about this little boy?" Dennis asked slowly. He wasn't sure he wanted to hear what Joe might say next. Had he fathered a child outside the marriage? Is that what the fight was about?

Joe hesitated with his answer as he faced a moral warfare in his head. "He's Marsha's nephew from

Memphis," he lied, losing the battle with his conscience. "We brought him back with us last night when we passed through there. He was supposed to spend a few weeks with us while school was out." Joe paused while he searched for more pieces to his story.

"So what happened?" asked Dennis, breaking the silence.

"He turned out to be a handful, and I wanted to take him back home," Joe answered.

"But he was only here for a day?" Dennis responded with a puzzled look.

"I know," Joe said shaking his head. "But I guess I'm just not used to kids being around. Look, Marsha was really furious about the whole thing because she didn't want her sister getting mad at us. So she just took the boy and stormed out of here," Joe said quickly. He was now feeling guilty for lying to Dennis, but he still wasn't ready to face the truth.

"Have you called her sister?" Dennis asked.

"Well, uh, no," Joe answered. "I hadn't thought about it. I just called you first."

"Marsha might have just decided to take the boy back home herself," said Dennis.

"But she didn't take anything with her."

"Look, Joe, I really don't think you need to get the police involved. I mean, you said she just left a few minutes ago. Like I said before, she just needs to go somewhere and calm down. She'll be back."

"Well, Dennis, it's really more serious than that," Joe said, realizing that his lie was getting him nowhere.

Dennis responded with a puzzled look.

"You know we've been trying to have a baby for years, then Marsha had that miscarriage or whatever you want to call it," Joe said with a sigh. "Well, she just hasn't been herself since, and she's been acting very irrationally lately."

"I still don't see why you needed to call the police."

"Because I'm afraid she might do something crazy," Joe answered emotionally.

"Don't take this the wrong way, man," said Dennis, "but I think you're the one doing something crazy. Calling the police because your wife left after a fight? C'mon, Joe, you know she'll be back in a little bit."

Joe knew Marsha wouldn't be back anytime soon. He had seen the look in her eyes when she'd said he would take Joshua over her dead body.

"Can't you at least put out a search for her or something?" Joe asked desperately.

"You know I can't," Dennis answered. "She's not even missing, Joe. But if it makes you feel any better, I'll keep an eye out for her car while I'm out tonight and I'll tell some of my buddies to do the same, okay?"

"Thanks, man," Joe said with a half smile.

"Now why don't you just relax and wait for your wife to come home," said Dennis.

Joe shrugged. "I'll try."

# FIFTEEN

"Do you think Joe will be mad at us?" Joshua asked as he leaned back in the leather seat of Marsha's sports car, his hands clasped behind his head.

Marsha smiled and shook her head. "Don't worry about Joe," she said. "He'll get over it. Like I told you before, we're just going on a short trip until Joe comes to his senses, okay?"

Joshua nodded. "Where are we going?" he asked.

"Oh, what do you think of Disney World?" Marsha asked teasingly.

"Disney World!" Joshua beamed. "You mean like with Mickey Mouse and all those other guys?"

"That's the one," Marsha answered proudly.

"Awesome!" cried Joshua, although he thought it was odd how he could remember things like Disney World and PlayStation, but not his own name. He could remember other things too, like pizza was his favorite food and "Hey, Arnold" was his favorite show and that he didn't like watching soap operas. But he couldn't remember anything about himself or what had happened in the woods.

The dead girl was still fresh on his mind too. He wondered who she was and what he had done to her. The police had probably found her by now and found his fingerprints all over her body. They were probably flying over the city in helicopters looking for him right now. But they'd never find him, he thought. He was on his way to Disney World. The cops would never spot him in that crowd.

"Isn't Disney World in Florida?" he asked.

"Yep," Marsha answered.

"Is that a long way from here?"

"A very long way," replied Marsha.

Joshua relaxed deeper into the seat. He was a free man.

———

By the time the ambulance and the police arrived, Terrence had calmed down enough to think to remove the backpack out of his closet and hide it under his bed. He didn't know how Jesse had found out about it or why he'd kept quiet until now. He was just glad it was still there and everything was still in it. He knew he would have to get rid of it soon. He'd decided he no longer wanted to be a part of Jay's troubles.

Jesse was still unconscious and lying on the floor in Terrence's bedroom. Terrence had wrapped a T-shirt around his head to slow down the bleeding. The once dingy white T-shirt was now drenched with blood. Terrence checked Jesse's pulse. It was still beating, but slowly. Jesse was barely breathing.

Terrence heard a loud knock at the door and ran to let the paramedics in.

"He's in here," Terrence said in a panicky voice as he led the paramedics to his bedroom.

Two paramedics and a cop followed Terrence into the bedroom. The paramedics rushed over to Jesse. The cop flipped out a notepad.

"What's your name, kid?" he asked routinely.

"Terrence McGee."

"And who's he? Your dad?" the cop asked nodding toward Jesse.

"Jesse Davis. He's my foster parent."

"What happened?" the cop asked without emotion.

Terrence's voice was a little shaky but controllable. His pulse was racing wildly. He recounted the nightmare to the policeman, leaving out the part about the backpack now hidden under the bed.

"It was self-defense. I swear," said Terrence. "I didn't want to hurt him."

The cop was writing everything down as fast as Terrence could spill it out. One of the paramedics informed them that Jesse had a concussion but would be okay. He had lost a lot of blood because of the alcohol he'd been drinking. But he'd survive.

Terrence breathed a sigh of relief. The paramedics lifted Jesse onto the stretcher and carried him out to the ambulance.

"You need to come with me and make a statement," the cop informed Terrence.

"But I just told you it was self-defense."

"Of course," the cop answered indifferently. "But you still need to come with me. It's routine stuff, kid. Papers to sign and stuff like that," he said with a shrug.

While Terrence put on his shoes, the cop carefully placed the trophy into a bag then scanned the room for any more evidence. When Terrence was ready, the cop led the way to the squad car. They drove off without flashing lights and a siren.

# SIXTEEN

Marsha suddenly awoke and realized she had slept for hours rather than minutes. She had found herself exhausted after driving into the wee hours of the night and had pulled over at a truck stop to grab a few minutes of sleep. One of the eighteen-wheelers which had shielded her sports car from view was now gone. Marsha figured no one was probably looking for her across state lines anyway. No one knew she was headed to Florida.

Marsha turned on the radio, and Joshua stretched like a cat then opened his eyes.

"Good morning," Marsha said to him.

Joshua looked around and checked out the surroundings as if he had forgotten where he was.

"Where are we?" he asked.

"We've just barely made it into Florida."

"We're almost at Disney World?" Joshua asked excitedly.

"No," answered Marsha with a laugh. "We're still a long way from Orlando."

"Oh," responded Joshua.

"Are you hungry?"

"I'm starving," Joshua answered, holding his stomach. "I could eat a whole elephant right now."

"Luckily you won't have to eat an elephant," said Marsha. "We can grab something here," she said, nodding toward the building labeled "Jimmy's Truckstop and Restaurant – Open 24 Hours."

Joshua looked at the restaurant and the longhaired truckers going in and coming out. He thought of bottled fruit punch and stale ham and cheese sandwiches wrapped in plastic. "Could we like maybe go to McDonald's or something?" he asked.

"Would you rather do that?"

"Definitely."

"Well, let's at least get some gas and go potty, okay?"

"Okay," answered Joshua.


The timing was perfect. Marsha found a McDonald's just about the time breakfast was almost over. Joshua knew the Happy Meals would be fresh and hot, just the way he liked them. He and Marsha picked a quiet booth in the back of the restaurant, away from the crowd. Joshua tore into his food like a bulldozer into dirt while Marsha ate slowly and stared at him.

She hated running like a fugitive. She had done nothing wrong. She was only trying to save Michael, she told herself. Why should she have to give him up? Nature had played a cruel trick on her and was trying to make it up to her by sending her a son. She was sure of that.

He was the son she and Joe had always wanted. Why couldn't Joe see that? They could all be living as one happy family if he didn't want to mess things up by going to the police. The police couldn't solve everything, she reasoned.

"Hey, I need to ask you something," said Joshua as he played with his Happy Meal toy.

"Okay," said Marsha, taking a sip from her cola.

"Can little kids go to jail?" Joshua asked with a serious look.

"What?" Marsha asked with a curious frown.

"Okay, let's say I kill someone," said Joshua. "Then I run from the police and they don't find me for a long time – say a few months maybe. Can they still put me in jail?"

"What are you talking about?" Marsha asked laughing.

"I know a kid who did this," said Joshua. "He's a friend of mine."

"Oh, really," said Marsha teasingly.

"Yeah," said Joshua. "And the police haven't found him yet. And I was wondering what was gonna happen to him when they do."

"You make a good storyteller," said Marsha.

"I'm telling you the truth. Matter of fact, I think my friend went to Disney World."

"Oh yeah?"

"Yeah. And if I see him there, I want to tell him it's safe to go back home."

"Did you see this on TV?"

"No, it's the truth," Joshua answered quickly. "This really happened to my friend."

"What's your friend's name?" Marsha asked to throw him off.

"His name?" asked Joshua, looking puzzled.

"Yes, his name," Marsha repeated. "Your friend does have a name, right?"

"Oh, yeah," answered Joshua. "But I can't tell you unless I know he's safe."

Marsha began to laugh. "Okay, you can tell your friend that it's safe to come out of hiding," she said, trying to control her laughing.

"You know this for sure?" Joshua asked skeptically.

"Yes, I know this for sure," answered Marsha. "Little children don't go to jail, and children don't murder people either. Your friend just made this up."

"No he didn't. He's on his way to Disney World right now."

"And just how is he getting there?"

"Somebody's taking him, just like you're taking me."

"So," Marsha sighed. "Are you trying to tell me that you're a murderer, and I'm helping you escape from the police?"

"No way!" Joshua cried quickly. "I told you it was a friend of mine."

"Okay," Marsha said giving in. "If we see your friend at Disney World, we'll let him know that it's safe to go back home."

"You mean it?"

"I mean it," said Marsha.

Terrence was nervous about calling his social worker at home on the weekend, but she had told him he could call her at anytime if he had a problem. Today he definitely had a problem. He had to get out of that apartment before Jesse got out of the hospital.

The police had brought Terrence back home later that night after the fight. Jesse was in the hospital with a fractured skull and a concussion. He would be there a few days. Terrence had tried to straighten up the mess Jesse had made in his room. He checked under his bed again to make sure the backpack was still there. The whole gang thought it would be safe with him since there weren't that many people in his apartment to go snooping around. Little did they know that Jesse would be sober long enough to go nosing around Terrence's room. That was a close call. Terrence had double-checked the bag to make sure Jesse hadn't stolen anything. Surprisingly he hadn't.

Terrence dialed the number that his social worker, Mrs. Greenwald, had given him. He anxiously waited as the phone rang three times, wanting desperately to hang up after each ring. When Mrs. Greenwald answered, Terrence contemplated hanging up but thought about caller-id.

"This is Terrence," he finally said after hesitation.

"Oh, good morning, Terrence." Mrs. Greenwald's voice sounded surprised.

"I'm sorry for calling you on the weekend," said Terrence, "but I have a really big problem."

"It's okay, Terrence. You can call me anytime," said Mrs. Greenwald. "Remember that."

Mrs. Greenwald's concern nearly brought tears to Terrence's eyes. It was the first time since his parents left that he actually felt as if someone cared for him. Maybe Jesse did before he started drinking, but it was hard to tell by the way he treated him presently. He didn't even know whether he trusted the guys he called his friends. Maybe they were just his friends because he was bigger than any kid his age and everybody was afraid of him.

"Mrs. Greenwald, I need to go to a new foster home," Terrence said in a weak voice.

"Are things not working out with Mr. Davis?"

Terrence fought back tears. "He tried to kill me last night," he answered.

"What! How?"

Terrence told Mrs. Greenwald the story with a teary voice.

"My goodness! Are you okay, Terrence?" she asked.

"I'm fine. Jesse's the one in the hospital."

"We've got to get you out of there before you get hurt. I'll start looking for you a place the minute I get off the phone," said Mrs. Greenwald.

Terrence felt relief. He prayed he would go to a home with a nice old lady who liked to fry chicken and make homemade biscuits.

———————

When Marsha hadn't returned or called by morning, Joe knew he had to call Dennis Moorehouse and tell him the truth despite the consequences. At least, that way, the police would be out searching for her rather than waiting for her to return home. Joe felt childish for having lied in the first place. Lies only made a situation worse.

He tried Dennis at the station and was told that he was off until later in the evening. Joe didn't want to talk to another police officer, so he called Dennis at home.

"Dennis, it's me Joe," he said when Dennis finally interrupted the answering machine.

"Umm," Dennis groaned. He was still asleep.

"Hey, man, I hate to disturb you this way, but I just couldn't talk to anyone else," Joe said.

"Joe?" Dennis asked sleepily.

"Yeah, man, it's me."

"Oh, yeah, what's up?" asked Dennis in a hoarse drowsy voice.

"It's about Marsha," Joe replied hesitantly.

"She's not back yet?" Dennis asked, unable to control the shock in his voice.

"No," answered Joe. "And—"

"And what, Joe?"

"And I didn't tell you the truth last night either," Joe blurted out.

Dennis fell silent for a moment. "Okay, so what's the truth?" he finally asked after several seconds of uncomfortable silence.

"The truth is Marsha doesn't have a nephew from Memphis," Joe said with a sigh.

"Ooookay. Go on."

"But she does have a kid with her," said Joe.

Dennis said nothing.

Joe took a deep breath. "We found him on the highway the other night when we were on our way back home," he said, then paused. "And we brought him home with us."

"You did what!"

"I know it was stupid to bring him home, but the kid had been beaten by his father and…"

"Hey, hey, slow down, man," Dennis interjected. "You're confusing me here."

"Okay, when we found the boy, he said that his father had beaten him and left him on the highway," Joe said.

Joe heard a chuckle come over the phone line. "You're kidding me, aren't you?" Dennis asked.

"No, man, I'm serious," Joe said somberly.

Dennis fell into deathly silence.

"We didn't go to the police because the boy was too terrified."

"Terrified of what?" Dennis asked with anxiety in his voice.

"I think he might of said something about not wanting his dad to go to jail."

"And you listened to him?"

"Marsha and I decided to let him calm down before we went to the police. We were afraid he'd runaway from us if we took him to a hospital or the police. And yesterday when

I told Marsha that I was calling the police, she took the boy and ran."

"Joe, why didn't you tell me this last night?"

"I was trying to keep Marsha out of trouble. Dennis, I thought she'd come to her senses and bring the boy back by now."

"Did it ever occur to you that someone would eventually be looking for this child, if not the parents, the police?"

"I tried to tell her that, but she wasn't hearing it. Why do you think she ran? She's just been out of her mind since the pregnancy, and this kid showing up just made it worse. She doesn't want to lose him, Dennis."

Dennis sighed heavily. "We'll find them, Joe," he said. "We'll get a search going and make it national. Heaven only knows where they are. Have you checked with relatives?"

"I called her sister in Memphis just in case. I didn't tell her that Marsha was gone. I just chatted with her, and I could tell from her conversation that she has no idea what's going on."

"Well tell me some more about the kid then."

"I don't know a whole lot, Dennis. His name is Michael Jones. I think he's about six or seven, average size, medium complexion, about like Marsha's. And he had a big bruise on his face from where his dad hit him."

"He didn't say anything about his parents or where he lives?"

"We didn't bother asking. We were just too confused to think."

"You say his dad beat him and left him on the highway?" Dennis asked with a tone of disbelief.

"That's what he told us. And he was pretty scared too."

"Hum, I wonder if they'll report him missing then," Dennis said with a sigh. "Where did you pick him up?" he added.

"On I-55 somewhere near Grenada."

"So he's not even from here," commented Dennis.

"No," Joe answered, his disposition even more somber than when he first made the call. The more he talked, the more he and Marsha sounded like kidnappers.

"Look, Dennis," Joe said. "I'm sorry I didn't just come clean with you last night."

"Hey, I understand. You were thinking of your wife."

"What's gonna happen next, Dennis?"

"I don't know right now. I'm gonna get dressed and get down to the station and get to working on this right away. You just hang tight, Joe."

Joe breathed deeply. He didn't really care whether he would be charged with kidnapping. He was more concerned about Marsha and how she would handle all this.

"Dennis, make sure Marsha doesn't get hurt," he said.

"I will, Joe," Dennis promised.


Two hours later, Joe received a call from Officer Moorehouse.

"I checked with every police station between here and Memphis that's anywhere close to I-55," Dennis Moorehouse said, then paused.

"And?" asked Joe.

"And not one of them has a report of a missing kid named Michael Jones," Dennis reported with a sad overtone.

"But if the kid's dad abandoned him, he's surely not gonna report him missing, wouldn't you think?"

"Not necessarily. He'd report him missing just to cover his own tail."

"So what do we do now? Just wait?"

"Every station I called is helping check to see whether there have been any reports of a missing child around Michael's age in the last coupla days. In the meantime, we have put out an APB on Marsha. Of course, I had to give all the details of the case, Joe, for Marsha's sake."

"Yes, I understand," said Joe.

"Okay, I'll chat with you later, man."

"Thanks, Dennis."

Joe hung up the phone and sank into a chair. He felt hopeless as he reached for the TV remote. It was a curious thing, but he had a feeling that if a child was reported missing it would be in the news. He zipped from channel to channel hoping to find something, but the only news on at two in the afternoon was CNN. He couldn't hope to hear anything about a missing kid from Mississippi there.

# SEVENTEEN

Joe received another call from Dennis at three P.M. He had information about a missing seven-year-old in a town near Grenada. His name was Joshua Tanner.

"Do you think it's the same kid?" Joe asked.

"That's what we need you to tell us," answered Dennis. "Do you have email at home?"

"Yeah, sure," Joe answered, his heart racing.

"Good. I'm gonna email you this picture of the kid so we don't lose too much time identifying him, okay?"

"Okay," answered Joe, still spell-bound by the excitement.

"What's your email address?" asked Dennis.

"JHOP007 at YOURMAIL dot com," Joe replied.

"Okay, I'm sending it right now."

"Hold up. I've got a separate line for the computer. I can check it while we talk."

"Good," said Dennis.

Joe rushed into his office. He was already logged on to the internet. He had been looking for "missing child" sites on the web. He checked his email and saw that the one from Dennis was already there.

"I got it," he said.

Joe opened the email and nearly dropped the phone. The picture on the screen was the kid he knew as Michael Jones.

"Joe? Are you still there?"

"Uh, yeah, I'm here," Joe said weakly. "It's him."

"Good!" exclaimed Dennis.

"What about his parents?" asked Joe.

"The kid musta made the story up, Joe. He lives with his grandmother. She reported him missing Thursday afternoon," Dennis answered matter-of-factly. "The detective that I spoke to said they believe he might've witnessed a murder."

"A murder!"

Dennis recapped the story of the search for Joshua, which led to the discovery of Sandy Cassin's body. Joe was stunned. Vivid memories of the little boy stumbling along the highway flashed through his head. He looked at the picture on his monitor. There was no doubt that this was the kid who called himself Michael Jones. The kid who said his parents had left him on the highway. A kid who might have witnessed a murder? No wonder he was so scared. Someone was probably after him. And poor Marsha! What will become of her when she finds out that the child belongs to someone who cares for him? She'll be devastated.

"Dennis, what's gonna happen to Marsha?" Joe asked wearily as he tried to rub the tension from the back of his neck.

"Everybody knows that this was all a big misunderstanding."

"But what about the fact that she's run off with him?"

"Don't worry, Joe. Marsha won't be charged with kidnapping," Dennis promised.

"It really was just a mistake," Joe reiterated. "The kid was all dirty and beat up and scared. We just didn't know what to do. We didn't want to scare him more by taking him to the police. And now I see why he didn't want to go."

"It's okay, Joe," said Dennis. "Stop worrying. Let the police handle this. Marsha and the kid will be found, and everyone will be returned safely."

"I hope you're right," Joe replied, although he knew he and Marsha would both need therapy after this.

---

The sign read, "Orlando 50 miles," and Joshua was hysterical with excitement. Fifty miles to Disney World. Fifty miles to Mickey and friends. Fifty miles to freedom. Only one thing stood in his way – he needed to go to the restroom, badly.

Marsha had already stopped at least ten times for gas, snacks, and potty breaks. It was only a few miles. He could hold it. Joshua looked at the Sprite can resting in the cup holder. It only made the situation worse. Joshua crossed his legs thinking that would help, but it didn't.

"Are you okay?" Marsha asked when she noticed Joshua's watery eyes.

Joshua nodded.

"Do you have to go?"

Joshua shook his head.

"Yes you do. I'll stop at the next station," Marsha said with an irritated sigh.

"Okay," Joshua mumbled.

"Don't worry. Disney World will still be there," said Marsha.

Five miles later Marsha stopped at a truck stop. She parked her car between two trucks, just in case someone was looking for them. Joshua headed straight for the restroom while Marsha stocked up on more snacks. She grabbed two bags of Doritos, a bag of Oreos, a Diet Coke, and nothing for Joshua to drink. Joshua came out of the restroom and joined her.

"Where's my drink?" he asked.

"I didn't think you needed anything to drink," replied Marsha.

"Well, I only had to go so bad cause I had two Sprites and I didn't go to the bathroom the last time we stopped."

"I don't want to have to stop again," Marsha informed him.

"You won't. I promise," said Joshua. "So can I please have a Mountain Dew? Please?" he begged.

Marsha told him to get a Mountain Dew from the freezer and they headed to the cashier.

"Hey, I saw two arcade games in the back. Can I have seventy-five cents and play just one game right quick?" Joshua asked.

"We don't really have time, Michael."

"Please," Joshua began to beg again. "I haven't played anything since yesterday. I need to stay in practice."

"Oh, all right," Marsha answered. She smiled and gave him a dollar. Joshua ran back to the games while Marsha went to pay for the snacks and drinks.

Marsha placed the items on the counter and cleared her throat to the get the attention of the cashier who was busy watching TV.

"Will that be all for you, ma'am?" the cashier asked after ringing the items.

Marsha didn't answer. Her eyes were suddenly glued to the television screen. There was a newsbrief about a missing child and a woman. Marsha was captivated as the newscaster read, "Joshua Tanner disappeared late Thursday afternoon. He was picked up on I-55 by Joe and Marsha Hopkins. For some reason he has identified himself as Michael Jones. Joshua was last seen with Marsha Hopkins."

Two photos appeared on the screen. One was of Joshua, the other Marsha. Marsha didn't wait to hear anymore. She bolted for the back of the store where she grabbed Joshua from his game.

"Hey, I'm not done yet!" he yelled as he was being pulled through the store. "I was about to break a record!"

Marsha ignored both Joshua and the baffled cashier as she fled from the store. The tires of her sports car screamed as they burned against the pavement. Marsha and Joshua were on the run again.

"What was that all about?" asked Joshua, who was still working on his seat belt.

"Nothing," Marsha answered sharply.

"Nothing?" Joshua asked waving his hands. "You pulled me away from my favorite game for nothing?"

"We had to leave!" Marsha screamed. She rubbed her hand across her face and tried to calm down. "The cashier accused me of trying to cheat her, and I just got a little teed off, okay?"

"A little teed off? Seems to me you were more than just a little teed off. You wouldn't even let me finish my game."

"I'm sorry," Marsha said more gently, but her hands were still shaking. "I just had to get out of there."

"What about our food and my Mountain Dew?"

"We'll get you one later."

"Great," Joshua said with a sneer.

"Look, I said I'll get you one later, okay?" Marsha said sternly.

Joshua muttered an okay.

Marsha was in no mood to talk about sodas. She had much more important things on her mind. Like why this kid was calling himself Michael Jones when he was really Joshua Tanner? It didn't matter anyway. She wasn't giving him back. He belonged to her now. No one was going to separate them. Not Joe, not the police, nobody.

Joshua watched the road signs. They should've been closer to Orlando by now, but he hadn't seen a sign yet that had anything about Orlando on it.

"I think we might be going the wrong way," he informed Marsha.

"We're okay," Marsha answered indifferently.

"We should've seen a sign about Orlando by now, shouldn't we?"

Marsha shrugged. "I've changed my mind. We're not going to Orlando."

"What! Then where are we going?" Joshua asked in disbelief.

"I haven't decided yet," said Marsha, again with indifference.

"Why can't we go to Disney World?" asked Joshua, his voice about to break.

"We just can't," Marsha answered coldly. "So just sit back and relax and I'll let you know where we're going when I make up my mind."

Joshua shrank back into his seat. He knew this was too good to be true.

# EIGHTEEN

The cashier at the truck stop had been too busy ringing up orders and cleaning restrooms to catch her favorite show, but she hurriedly made her way back to the set just in time to catch the last ten minutes of the news. She might not know what's going on locally, but at least she could keep current with regional news, she reasoned.

The faces on the screen looked familiar to the cashier, and she thought about the woman who had rushed out of the store earlier that evening leaving her stuff on the counter.

"That was them!" she exclaimed to a customer who had come to the counter to pay for gas.

"Who?" asked the man at the counter.

"The woman and the boy on the news," the cashier answered, pointing toward the television. "They were in here earlier tonight."

The man leaned over the counter to catch a glimpse.

"That's why she ran out of here. I bet she kidnapped that little boy," the cashier said anxiously as she scribbled down the number on the screen.

"Wow," the man responded.

"No wonder the boy was trying to get away from her," she rattled on. "He tried to hide in the back in the arcade room, I think."

"Amazing," the man commented.

"I'm calling this number right now," said the cashier as she handed the man his change. "That little boy must be scared out of his wits," she added as she picked up the phone.

———————

Dwight Quattleman had just gotten home when the phone rang. It was Detective Briggs.

"Quattleman, the kid's been spotted," Briggs said excitedly.

"Where?"

"In Florida, near Orlando."

"Florida! Is he with the Hopkins woman?"

"Yes, according to the woman who called the hotline."

"What else do you know?" asked Quattleman.

"A cashier at a truck stop said they came in around seven, then the Hopkins lady just grabbed the kid and scatted like a cat in a room full of dogs."

"That was over four hours ago," Quattleman noted. "They could be anywhere by now."

"At least we know they're not in Mississippi," added Briggs. "The authorities in Florida are checking every hotel in and around Orlando to see whether they've checked in anywhere."

"Is anybody posting their pictures?"

"They're on that too."

"If the Hopkins picked up the kid by accident, why did she run out of the store the way the cashier says she did?" asked Quattleman.

"Beats me. Although the cashier did mention that the boy looked scared," Briggs added.

"This whole situation is making my head spin," said Quattleman. "Why hasn't Joshua tried to call his grandmother?"

"He's a kid, and he's scared," replied Briggs. "If he knows anything about the Cassin murder, then he knows that the police aren't the only ones looking for him. He got away from someone in those woods that afternoon."

"Yeah, I guess he wouldn't be in any hurry to get back home," said Quattleman.

"I'll stay on the phone with the folks in Florida," said Briggs. "You in for the night?"

"No way. I can't sleep now," answered Quattleman. "I'll see you in a little bit."

---

It was almost 1 A.M., and Marsha was completely wiped out from driving. Joshua had pestered her continuously about his Mountain Dew until he'd fallen asleep at midnight. Marsha was too scared to stop, but her gas tank was empty and she also knew that Joshua would wake up soon either wanting something to drink or something to eat. Plus

Marsha needed to stop and rethink her plans. She was tired of driving aimlessly along the East Coast.

She took her chances and stopped at a station somewhere near Savannah, Georgia. Before pulling up to the pump, Marsha drove close enough to the store to peep inside to see whether there was a TV set on the premises. There wasn't one. It was safe to stop.

A sign taped to the pump read, "Pay before pumping after 8 P.M." Unfortunately, the station had not updated to "pay at the pump" status. Marsha woke Joshua, who immediately asked about his Mountain Dew, and the two went inside for the usual – gas, snacks, and a potty break. Marsha returned from the restroom and collected the goodies – chips, cookies, a six-pack of Mountain Dew, and two plastic-wrapped ham and cheese sandwiches. "I'll have twenty dollars worth of super unleaded," she told the cashier as she placed her supplies on the counter.

"That'll be $30.02," the cashier informed her.

Marsha handed the cashier $31. She didn't want to take anymore chances using a credit card. She watched him closely to see whether he looked like he suspected anything. He didn't. He simply handed her her change and turned the pump on. Marsha took the money, and she and Joshua hastily left the store.

A teenager driving a Subaru had pulled up to the other side of the pump. He got out of the car, leaving the keys inside, and went in to prepay for his gas. Without thinking Marsha grabbed Joshua by the arm and ran toward the Subaru. "Get in!" she yelled as she ran to the driver's side.

Joshua pulled on the door. "It's locked!" he cried in a panicky voice, not knowing why he was getting into someone else's car anyway.

Marsha hopped in on the driver's side and reached over and unlocked the door for Joshua. Joshua opened the door and got in. Marsha turned on the ignition and floored the Subaru. Joshua sat wide-eyed, clutching the sack of goodies against his chest.

"Hey! That woman just stole my car!" the teenager yelled as he bolted for the door. "Come back here!" he yelled, fruitlessly chasing after the speeding car. He ran to the edge of the road and yelled a few unspeakables at the taillights of the car. The Subaru disappeared into the darkness.

The teenager rushed back into the store. "Call the police!" he ordered the cashier. "My car's been stolen!"

The cashier dialed the police and reported the stolen car. He then turned to the bewildered teenager and said with a grin, "Look at it this way, kid. She traded you a Corvette for a Subaru, and she's already paid for a full tank of gas. I'd say it's Christmas in July."

"Very funny. That's my dad's car, and I'm not even supposed to be driving it," the teenager replied. "But she won't get too far. It doesn't have any gas in it."

Both Marsha and Joshua had been silent for five minutes. Joshua was squeezing the life out of the sack while Marsha watched the gas hand sail past the "E." She knew she couldn't drive much farther.

"Why did we steal this car?" Joshua finally asked through trembling lips.

"We didn't steal it," answered Marsha. "We just borrowed it for a while."

"Then why did we borrow it without asking?"

"Because we needed another car."

"Why?"

"Because the police are after us. That's why," Marsha snapped.

"The police!" exclaimed Joshua. *That's why we couldn't go to Disney World*, he thought. *I wonder if she knows why they're after us. I bet they found the body and my fingerprints and blood and everything. But how did they know I was with Marsha? Joe! I bet he told them everything!*

"How do you know the police are after us?" Joshua asked cautiously.

"I saw our picture on TV tonight when we were in Florida at the truck stop."

"Is that why we turned around?"

"Yes. But it's for your own good," Marsha added quickly.

"Did the police say anything like why they're after me, I mean us?"

Marsha shrugged. "I didn't hear the whole thing," she answered. It didn't matter to Marsha anyway. If Joshua didn't want to go home to his lousy family, then he didn't have to as far as she was concerned. They would eventually find a place to stop. They could change their identities, and no one would be the wiser. Plenty of missing children never returned home. Joshua would just be one of them, except he would have a better home.

"So they just showed our pictures on TV and nothing else?" Joshua asked.

"That's all I saw," Marsha answered.

Joshua loosened his grip on the sack. *She still doesn't know anything,* he thought. *If I can just keep her away from the TV, she'll keep running with me forever. She'll never know she's running with a murderer.*

———————

Quattleman had been on the phone talking back and forth with the Florida police. They had obtained nothing on the Tanner kid's whereabouts. Every hotel within a 100-mile radius of Orlando had been checked, and no woman with a young boy had checked into any of them.

Quattleman's phone rang. It was the Georgia police. "This is Dwight Quattleman," he answered.

"This is Officer Danny Hewlett with the Georgia police. I just got back from answering a complaint about a stolen car, and after a series of phone calls I was connected to you. We found out that the car was stolen by a woman named Marsha Hopkins."

Quattleman bolted upright in his chair. "Is the kid still with her?" he asked anxiously.

"He was at the time the car was stolen. I believe that she might be headed north on interstate 95. We've notified the South Carolina highway patrol. They'll be looking out for her."

"We'll need to update our APB," said Quattleman. "What kind of car is she driving now?"

"A white 1997 Subaru Legacy."

Quattleman wrote down the information. "Thanks for your help," he said.

"Good luck," responded Hewlett.

# NINETEEN

Marsha had begun to get nervous. The little gas tank symbol was blinking, and there wasn't a station in sight. Joshua was busy with his snacks and had no idea that he might be walking at any moment. Marsha glanced over at Joshua. It was so unfair that they had to run like fugitives. All the kid wanted was to be happy and live a normal life, and all she wanted was to give him that life.

Marsha saw flashing blue lights in her rearview mirror. She looked at the speedometer. She wasn't speeding. Her heart sank, and a wave of fear swept over her body. She sped up and so did the marked car with the flashing lights. She looked at the gas hand and panicked. She was literally riding on air. Nevertheless, she floored the Subaru.

Kevin Smith, a South Carolina highway patrolman, had received the call only minutes before to be on the lookout for a stolen 1997 Subaru Legacy. But a confrontation with a car thief was the last thing he wanted to deal with at 1:30 A. M. He called for backup.

With a greasy face, Joshua finally looked up from his Doritos bag. "What's going on?" he asked.

"We're being chased," Marsha answered calmly.

"You mean like on 'Cops?'" Joshua asked with a grin.

"This isn't a game, Michael," Marsha said firmly.

"You're telling me," he said, looking back over his seat. "Wow, we must be going a hundred miles per hour. Do you think he'll catch us?"

Marsha didn't have to answer Joshua's question. The car spoke for itself. It started decelerating.

"Why are we slowing down?" Joshua asked in a panicky voice. "He'll catch us. Can't you speed up?"

Marsha had no choice but to pull over. But she wasn't giving up that easily, not without a fight. She was not letting Joshua go back to be abused again.

Kevin pulled the patrol car onto the shoulder of the highway behind the Subaru. He saw another patrol car coming behind him, so he waited for it before he got out. The other patrol car pulled up behind Kevin's. Kevin got out and walked up to the driver's side of the Subaru. He was about to ask Marsha to see her license, but he was panic-stricken as he looked through the window. There sat Joshua shaking uncontrollably on the passenger's side with a pistol pointed at him.

"Stand back!" Marsha ordered through clenched teeth. "Do as I say, or I'll shoot him."

Kevin stepped back.

"I need some gas," Marsha informed him. "And you're gonna get it for me."

Kevin was dumbfounded. "What ever you say, ma'am," he answered with caution. "I need to check with my partner back there," he said, motioning toward the other car. "We'll see what we can do."

"Don't try anything funny," Marsha commanded. "I'm not kidding. I will shoot him."

Kevin ran back to the other car while trying to consider what to do next without risking Joshua's life.

In the meantime Marsha was busy trying to convince Joshua that she wasn't really going to shoot him but just needed to scare the patrolmen. Joshua wasn't convinced, however, not as long as there was a pistol pointed at him. He didn't think he could ever trust this woman again, not after seeing her whisk that pistol out of that big purse of hers and point it at him. Joe had given Marsha the pistol for protection. It wasn't even loaded.

Joshua began to cry.

"Please don't cry," Marsha pleaded. "I'd never hurt you like your daddy. This is just until we get the gas."

Joshua was speechless. He couldn't stop shaking and couldn't stop the tears.

"After they fill up the tank, we'll go on to Disney World, okay?" Marsha said, trying to sound cheerful.

Joshua didn't want to go to Disney World anymore. He didn't want to go anywhere with Marsha. She was crazy. He'd rather take his chances with the police. At least they wouldn't point a gun to his head. There was no way he was going any farther with this lunatic, he thought, even if it meant going to prison.

Marsha kept her eyes on the rearview mirror, and Joshua kept his eyes on Marsha as he carefully inched his trembling hand closer to the door handle. When his hand reached the door, Joshua quickly jerked the handle and jumped out of the car. He scrambled on his hands and knees trying desperately to get away from the car as fast as he could.

"Stay down!" Kevin yelled as he rushed toward Joshua.

The other patrolman ordered Marsha to surrender. She stepped out of the car with her hands up. She knew it was all over. There was no need to put up a fight.

"Are you hurt?" Joshua heard Kevin ask.

"No, Sir," Joshua answered, shaking his head and crying.

Kevin picked him up and carried him to the patrol car. "You're safe now, son," he said.

# TWENTY

Detective Briggs was on the phone as Quattleman stood by and waited. They both had been busy all night keeping track of what was going on on the East Coast. "I want Joshua Tanner on a plane to Memphis as soon as the sun comes up," he told the policeman on the other end. "We'll be there waiting for him. We've got a murderer on the loose here, and that kid will put him behind bars," he said before he hung up the phone.

"Yes!" Quattleman shouted as he and Briggs gave each other high-fives. "Maybe I'll be able to get some sleep by tomorrow," he added.

"Maybe this whole city will be able to get some sleep once we find Sandy Cassin's killer," said Briggs.

––––––––––

Joshua arrived in Memphis at 8 A.M. Quattleman and Briggs were waiting for him. Joshua had now gathered enough information from the police to know that his name was Joshua Tanner. They wouldn't tell him a whole lot, but Joshua also knew by now that he wasn't wanted for murder. That became obvious to him when Kevin didn't handcuff him or shove him by the head into the backseat of the patrol car. Joshua also realized how crazy the thought was anyway that he could've killed someone twice his size. Besides, there was blood all over the body and he didn't even have a murder weapon.

Joshua wasn't sure whether he was looking forward to the long ride in the car with two more policemen. They had told him it would take over an hour to get home, or at least to the police station. Joshua wasn't allowed to go home until the murderer was behind bars, he was told. "Someone has obviously tried to take you out once already," Briggs had informed him. "We can't let anybody know you're back in town, not even your grandma," he had said.

"You're gonna be a hero, Joshua," Quattleman said as he looked back at Joshua through the rearview mirror.

"A hero? How?"

"As soon as you nail the creep who killed the girl in the woods," answered Briggs.

"Who? Me?" Joshua asked.

"Yes, little man, you," replied Briggs.

Joshua wished he could melt himself into the seat. He wished he could go back one day in time and be back at Marsha's before she went psycho. Everything was good there. They had a nice house with a big yard. There was a dog to play with and a new PlayStation. Marsha took him shopping and let him eat whatever he wanted. And most of all there was no killer on the loose looking for him.

Joshua closed his eyes and pretended to sleep. He heard Quattleman ask a question, but he didn't answer. He didn't even move. He made sure he breathed like a sleeping person, in and out, very slowly, not missing a beat.

"He must be terrified," Joshua heard Briggs say. "Who knows what happened to him in the woods, then to get kidnapped by that crazy woman from Jackson," he said shaking his head.

"Did they lock her up?" Quattleman asked.

"No," answered Briggs. "Her husband flew to Savannah to get her, I was told. He's admitting her to a psychiatric clinic in Jackson."

"Well, at least that part of the nightmare is over for Joshua," Quattleman commented.

"What do you mean 'that part of the nightmare?'" Briggs inquired.

"What if he can't identify the killer?" asked Quattleman. "Or what if the killer has left town?"

"Oh, yeah, I see what you mean," said Briggs. "The poor kid and his grandma could be living in fear for who knows how long."

Joshua swallowed to get the lump out of his throat. His situation was worse than he'd thought. He should've kept running with Marsha, or maybe he should just come clean with the truth.

---

Joshua had finally fallen asleep after pretending for half an hour. When he awoke, he saw that they had arrived at the police station. Quattleman opened the door for him, and he and Briggs escorted him through the back of the station into an office.

"Did you say the killer might be still looking for me?" Joshua asked Briggs who was anxiously pacing the floor .

"It's likely," Briggs answered.

"What if I don't remember anything?" Joshua asked. "Would he still come after me?"

"I don't think the killer is gonna buy that story. It's the oldest trick in the book. You'll be a dead duck before you even make it home," said Briggs, who was now trying to intimidate Joshua.

"What if I really don't remember anything? Why would anybody want to kill me then?"

"Because one day you will remember," answered Briggs.

"Joshua, are you saying you don't know what happened to Sandy Cassin?" Quattleman interjected.

"Maybe," answered Joshua.

"What do you mean 'maybe?'" asked Briggs.

"Maybe I don't remember anything," answered Joshua.

"That's ridiculous," Briggs said with a nervous laugh.

"Why don't you tell us what you do remember, Joshua," said Quattleman.

"Let's say I can't remember what happened," Joshua proposed. "Will you guys still protect me from the killer?"

"We won't know who the killer is if you can't remember anything," said Briggs. "As far as we know the killer could be your next door neighbor, then the next thing we know you've got your little throat slashed."

Joshua jumped.

"Quit trying to scare him, Chuck," said Quattleman.

"Hey, it's the truth. How are we gonna protect him if he doesn't know anything?"

"Okay, okay. I'll tell you what I know," Joshua said quickly.

"Okay, out with it," ordered Briggs.

"Well. Uh. I. Uh."

"Look, Joshua, do you want us to protect you or not?" asked Briggs.

"I do. I do," Joshua answered quickly. "Okay. I was in the woods. And, uh, I saw a girl and a man. Yeah, I saw a girl and a man. And they were fighting. You know, like they were lovers or something."

"Lovers?" asked Quattleman.

"Yeah, you know, like boyfriend and girlfriend."

"Yeah, sure," said Briggs, who glanced a look of suspicion toward Quattleman. Quattleman returned the look. "What happened next?"

"Uh, the girl slapped the man like in the movies, and the man hit her and knocked her to the ground," said Joshua. "Then he killed her."

"How?" asked Briggs.

Joshua thought about the blood. "Uh, with a knife," he answered.

"Did the man see you?" asked Briggs.

"No."

"So how did you get the bruise?"

"I fell."

"You fell, huh," Briggs commented. "Okay enough with the games, Joshua. Why won't you just tell us what happened? Were you even in the woods on Thursday afternoon?" Briggs asked impatiently.

Joshua nodded.

"Did you see Sandy Cassin?"

Joshua nodded again.

"What do you remember about her?"

Joshua looked sheepish. "She was already dead when I remember seeing her," he answered.

Briggs stopped pacing and sat down. He rested his face in the palms of his hands. "Joshua, let's start over, okay?"

Joshua answered with a nod.

"Did you see the person who killed Sandy Cassin?" Briggs asked.

"No," Joshua mumbled.

Briggs jumped up from the chair and waved his arms through the air. "We've gone through all this trouble to save you from a kidnapper, driven all the way to Memphis to pick you up and fed you at McDonalds, and you don't know anything?"

"Cut it out, Chuck," Quattleman ordered. "The boy just can't think with all your yelling."

"I need to tell you something," interrupted Joshua.

"What is it, Joshua?" asked Quattleman.

"I think I have like amnesia or something."

"That's when people forget who they are," Briggs said. "You know who you are," he said sharply.

"But I didn't before the policeman told me."

"Yeah, right," Briggs sneered.

"Do you remember your grandmother, Joshua?" asked Quattleman.

"A little bit since you started talking about her."

"Then what do you remember?" Briggs interjected.

"I remember waking up in the woods, and my head was hurting," Joshua began. "I couldn't remember how I got there or anything. I was scared so I started running. No, wait, I started crawling first. That's when I fell on the girl."

"So you are telling the truth about seeing her?" asked Quattleman.

"Yeah. Then I got up and ran. I just kept running till I got to the highway. Then Joe and Marsha picked me up."

Quattleman rubbed his forehead hoping to ease some of the tension. "So you don't remember anything prior to waking up in the woods?" he asked.

"No," Joshua answered shaking his head.

"So what are we supposed to do now?" Briggs said to Quattleman. "Hit him over the head so he'll get his memory back?" he asked facetiously.

"This isn't a joke, Chuck. We've got to get him to a doctor."

"Then let's do it quickly," said Briggs. "We've wasted enough time already."

---

Dr. Isaac Denton arrived at the station twenty minutes after Briggs called the hospital. Briggs had made it clear to the hospital that he needed a psychiatrist right away and any delays would be considered an obstruction of justice. He and Quattleman didn't want to take any chances on Joshua being seen by the public, so they opted to have him checked out in Briggs's office.

"We need him cured pronto," Briggs announced when he greeted the doctor at the reception desk. "He has amnesia," he added.

"Amnesia?" the doctor asked with a curious glance.

"He got hit on the head, and he can't remember anything," Briggs said. "So you just need to hit him again and he'll remember, right?"

"No," answered the doctor shaking his head. "It's not that simple. We first need to see what's wrong with him."

"You're the doctor," Briggs answered sarcastically.

When they reached the office, the doctor took a seat directly in front of Joshua. "Why don't we start by telling me what's happened to you, Joshua," he said.

Joshua retold the story that he'd told Quattleman and Briggs.

"Now," began Dr. Denton, "it's very important that you answer this next question correctly, Joshua."

Joshua nodded that he understood.

"When did you realize that you had lost your memory?" asked Dr. Denton.

"When did I realize it?" repeated Joshua.

"Yes. Was it when you woke up or was it when someone asked you your name?"

"Let's see," said Joshua. "When I first woke up, I was just scared. I didn't really think about remembering anything. I guess I really didn't know there was something wrong with me until Joe asked me my name."

"What are you getting at, Dr. Denton?" asked Quattleman.

"Joshua doesn't have amnesia," the doctor answered.

"He doesn't?" Briggs asked.

"Then what do I have?" asked Joshua. "I don't remember anything."

"You have a loss of memory, but it's temporary," answered the doctor. "You've had a traumatic experience that you've chosen to block from your memory. In the process you've also blocked out other important information such as your name."

"Are you sure about this, Dr. Denton?" asked Briggs.

"Yes, I'm sure," replied Dr. Denton. "It's the same type of memory blockage a war veteran or a person who suffered abuse as a child might experience, except Joshua has blocked out his short-term memory."

Briggs shook his head in disbelief.

"Detective Briggs," said Dr. Denton, "haven't you ever studied for an exam, then gone totally blank when the test was placed in front of you?"

"Well, yes."

"The memory loss may be brief such as during an examination or a speech, or it may be long-term such as an abuse case or trauma."

"Okay, then how do we cure him?" asked Briggs.

"Sometimes the patient will cure himself when he's ready to accept what he has experienced. At that point he'll remember everything that he thinks he has forgotten."

"We don't have time for that," said Briggs.

"The other option is hypnosis," said Dr. Denton.

"You mean like with a necklace?" Joshua asked.

"No, Joshua," replied Dr. Denton. "Hypnosis is just a relaxed state of mind. It's just like when you're watching cartoons or playing video games, and you aren't aware of anything else that's going on around you."

"So will you put me to sleep?"

"Kinda."

"Awesome!"

# TWENTY-ONE

Terrence lay in bed and stared at the ceiling. He should have been smiling. He had received a call from Mrs. Greenwald at eight o'clock, and she had informed him that she'd found him another home. She would be picking him up at ten. But no smile came to his lips. Sure he would be away from Jesse and his troubles, but he still had reality to face. Sandy Cassin was dead. Murdered by him and his friends.

Jay should've never gotten involved with her, Terrence thought. He knew that Sandy had tricked Darrell into selling drugs for her boyfriend from New York. What made him think she was telling the truth when she said she knew how to get Darrell and Stephen out of jail? Did he really think that Sandy's boyfriend could pull strings for them? It was all just a lie to get Jay to sell drugs for them.

Terrence got up and got the backpack from under his bed. He poured the money out onto his bed. He didn't know what to do with it. He wished Jesse would've just stolen it for him. Stupid drug money. Money that belonged to some of his own neighbors. Money that people should've used to pay bills, buy food, or clothes for their kids.

Terrence put the money back into the backpack. Jay was supposed to give it to Sandy at the pond, but things didn't go as planned. Sandy started teasing Jay about how he was just as stupid as his brothers, how the police would be knocking on his door soon because word was out again that drugs were moving through the projects. She said that she and her boyfriend didn't have anymore use for him because he wasn't discreet enough with his work. Jay had begged her not to turn him in, then Ron threatened her with his knife. The rest of them had joined in to try to scare her into getting her and her boyfriend to back off Jay. That's when Jay accidentally pushed Sandy into Ron's knife. No one would ever believe it was an accident now.

---

Dr. Denton had dimmed the lights in the office and turned on some classical music in order to help Joshua relax. "I want you to forget that you are at the police station, Joshua," he said. "Forget about the road trip you took with Mrs. Hopkins. I want you to think about being in a pleasant place like a park."

Joshua closed his eyes and nodded in obedience. Briggs had brought a bench into the office so that Joshua could lie down during the hypnosis. Joshua lay in his favorite position on his back with his hands behind his head.

Dr. Denton allowed Joshua to listen to the music for a while before he began talking. He had come equipped with a cassette of classical music commonly used in cartoons. He had used it before on children who were able to listen to the music and quickly fall into the same trance that they fell into while watching TV. "Now, Joshua," Dr. Denton began in a whisper, "I want you to try to think back to last Thursday afternoon."

Joshua nodded.

"Joshua, I want you to go to the woods behind your apartment complex," said Dr. Denton.

"Okay," Joshua said quietly.

"Where are you, Joshua?" asked Dr. Denton.

"I'm.... I'm in the woods."

"What are you doing in the woods?"

"I came to swim."

"Do you see the pond?"

"Yes."

"Do you see a girl?"

"No."

Briggs looked at Quattleman and commented with a grunt.

"What do you see, Joshua?" asked Dr. Denton.

"I see trees."

"And the pond?"

Joshua nodded.

Dr. Denton let out a sigh. Briggs was about to say something, but Dr. Denton motioned to him to keep quiet. "Joshua, are you at the pond?" he asked.

Joshua didn't answer.

Dr. Denton repeated his question.

"I've got to get outta here," Joshua whispered.

"Why, Joshua?" asked Dr. Denton.

"They're coming up the path."

"Who's coming up the path?"

"Terrence 'nem."

"I…I was going for a swim. I didn't see nothing. I swear," Joshua muttered.

"Great," Briggs muttered under his breath. "We're right back where we started."

"Shhh!" Dr. Denton commanded.

"Just leave me alone," Joshua said nearly sobbing.

"We can wake him up now," said Dr. Denton.

"He hasn't told us anything yet," said Briggs.

"He will when he wakes up," said Dr. Denton. "Turn on the lights please."

Quattleman turned on the lights, and Joshua opened his eyes.

"It's okay, Joshua," said Dr. Denton. "You're safe now."

# TWENTY-TWO

It was almost ten o'clock and Terrence had packed everything he owned, including the backpack. He figured he would hold on to it until Jay got out of the hospital, then he'd let him figure out what to do with it. He sat on the worn sofa in the living room and made a vow that he would stay out of trouble. He promised himself that he would study hard and do better in school. He owed it to Mrs. Greenwald and the family who was taking him in. Terrence jumped when he heard a knock at the door. He was more than anxious to open it. He was ready to leave his old life behind.

"Are you all packed and ready?" Mrs. Greenwald asked.

"Definitely," Terrence answered.

"Well let's get your things and go."

"I just have these two pieces," Terrence said. He'd had them sitting by the door.

As they headed out of the apartment, Terrence stopped cold when he saw the police cruiser parked behind Mrs. Greenwald's Impala. Briggs and another officer approached him.

"Terrence McGee?" Briggs inquired.

Terrence knew that the officers knew who he was. It was just a formality. He knew what lay ahead of him. He knew that he had to pay the consequences for his foolishness. He knew that the emotional nightmare was finally over. "Yes, I'm Terrence McGee," he answered politely, remembering his vow to change his ways.

"You're under arrest for the murder of Sandy Cassin," Briggs stated. "You have the right to remain silent...."

Terrence didn't hear the rest. He was looking at Ron and Allen in the backseat of the car. They were both crying. Terrence felt sorry for them.

"What's going on, Officer?" asked Mrs. Greenwald, her forehead furrowed in disbelief.

The other officer explained what was going on to Mrs. Greenwald while Briggs handcuffed Terrence and led him to the car. "Thank you, Mrs. Greenwald," Terrence said over his shoulder as he was being placed into the car.

---

Joshua felt both joy and fear as Quattleman's car approached Sadie Belle's apartment. He couldn't wait to see his grandmother again, but he also wondered whether she would be angry with him for sneaking to the pond. When the car stopped, he hesitated to open the door.

"What's the matter?" Quattleman asked.

"What if Grandma's mad at me?"

"Are you kidding? She's been worried sick over you. Of course she's not mad."

But before Joshua could get the door opened, Sadie Belle had already come running out of the apartment. Her neighbor Jackie and Marvin and his mother followed her.

"Joshua!" they all screamed excitedly.

"Have mercy!" Sadie Belle cried as she yanked opened the door of Quattleman's car. "My grandbaby is safe," she said with her eyes full of tears.

"Grandma!" Joshua screamed as he jumped out of the car and into Sadie Belle's arms. "Grandma, please don't be mad at me," Joshua pleaded. "I'm sorry I lied to you," he said as tears streamed down his face.

"Boy, hush yo' mouth," Sadie Belle said as she held Joshua securely in her arms. "I'm just glad you're safe at home again."

"Me too, Grandma," Joshua said between sobs. "I love you, Grandma."

"I love you too, Baby," said Sadie Belle.

"Grandma," Joshua said as he looked up at Sadie Belle. "Can we watch 'Oprah' today?"

Made in the USA